# THE CRUMB

Jean Slaughter Doty

# THE CRUMB

Greenwillow Books
A DIVISION OF
WILLIAM MORROW &
COMPANY, INC.
NEW YORK

3  4  5

Library of Congress Cataloging in Publication Data
Doty, Jean Slaughter (date)    The crumb.
Summary: A young girl and her pony become involved in the horse
show circuit when she gets a job helping out at a nearby stable and
riding school.
1. Ponies—Legends and stories.    [1. Ponies—Fiction.    2. Horse
shows—Fiction]    I. Title.
PZ10.3.D7197Cr    [Fic]    75-33648
ISBN 0-688-80035-1    ISBN 0-688-84035-3 lib. bdg.

To R.D.
for his incredible patience
and encouragement

# Chapter 1

**T**wilight was gathering in the hollows between the fields as I rode through the farm gate, latched it shut, and set my pony into a canter. The track ahead of us led over the crest of the hill and sloped unevenly down to the woods below. It was dry up on the top of the hill where the March winds had blown all day over the crumpled grass, which was just beginning to turn green. The footing was good, not heavy with mud as it was in the hollows, and The Crumb galloped eagerly and joyfully into the wind, with me hanging on for dear life and loving every minute of it.

I coaxed the pony back into a walk, eventually—to be absolutely honest, he didn't have the softest mouth in the world and pulling him up from a gallop wasn't always easy—but he was fat and puffing from a winter's idle pleasures, and so he didn't give me any argument as he jogged peacefully down the other side of the hill.

I wiggled into a more comfortable position on his bare back and surveyed my kingdom with satisfaction. It consisted of a generous amount of open fields and woods to ride in and one rather-too-plump dun pony, whose official name was Buttercrumb Cake, so of course I called him The Crumb. He was big—just a shade under fourteen-two hands, almost as tall as a small horse. Like all duns, he had a black mane and tail and black legs and the traditional black stripe down his back, and in the summer, after he'd finished shedding out, his coat was a heavenly shade of honey gold.

If you're like me and have a passion for riding and ponies and horses, now that you know what The Crumb looked like, you'll probably want to know where he came from and how I came to have him. It's sort of like seeing a horse van or a trailer go by—I always ache to stop it and look inside and find out whose horses they are and where they're going, and certainly where they came from—so I'll have to confess quickly that I don't know an awful lot about The Crumb.

I do know he spent some part of his life in a riding academy, that he'd been fox hunting and had certainly played polo somewhere along the way. When I got him the vet said the pony was slightly on the heavenward side of fourteen years old (which could mean just about anything from fifteen to eighteen, and if he was older than that, I didn't want to know), and after I got him he was Junior Jumper champion at our county show two years in a row. (This either speaks well for The Crumb, my father says, or not very highly of his competition, depending on your point of view.)

As these wonderful things sometimes happen, even in real life, the people who owned him last wanted to retire the pony; this only meant that their children wanted to go on to what they considered to be bigger and better things, such as Thoroughbred show hunters and such, and, one way or another, he found his way to me.

For the last three years I baby-sat and did this and that to keep The Crumb warm and well fed and properly shod, and we had a wonderful time.

It was darker down in the woods when we reached them, but The Crumb was clever on his feet and he walked along the narrow path without any trouble. There was no wind down here in the hollow. The woods were heavy with the smell of early spring. Though we were not far from home, these back acres of the old farm could have been a million miles from nowhere and The Crumb and I came here often on our short rides after school.

The path turned and led toward a gap in the stone wall. The stream behind us was roaring with the overflow of the heavy March rains; I suppose this is why neither The Crumb nor I heard the horse van before we saw its headlights dipping and weaving across the open field on the other side of the wall.

Crumb threw his head in the air and shied and I nearly fell off. I grabbed a handful of mane to keep myself from sliding over his shoulder. It would have been much easier, of course, just to flip off onto my feet, but this kind of thing never occurs to me in the middle of the complications of trying to stay on— I think about it afterward, when I already feel like a fool and it's much too late.

Finally, after an awful lot of scrambling and clutching, I worked myself back to where I belonged and gave Crumb a cross jerk on the reins. This was unfair. It wasn't his fault I'd been riding so sloppily that I'd nearly gone off. I patted him apologetically on the shoulder and he tossed his head once or twice, but he forgave me as he always did—he was a very forgiving pony—and he stood still, snorting quietly, at the gap in the wall.

Naturally we'd both seen a horse van before, but we were not exactly prepared to see one in the back cow pasture of Mr. Martin's farm, lurching its way toward us over the uneven ground. Even though it was quite dim in the woods, there was more daylight in the open field, and I could see that the van was a sleek and shining model, painted a dark cherry red, but I couldn't read the name of the owner lettered in white beside the door. Above the low straining of the engine I could hear the thud of hoofs as a horse in the van moved a little to keep its balance.

I backed my pony deeper into the woods and waited. It was really peculiar, seeing this elegant van grinding its way across a hidden cow pasture in the almost-dark, and the proverbial wild horses (what there are left of them) couldn't have dragged me away until I found out what was going on.

The van stopped. A man's voice called out "Whoa!" as the horse's hoofs clattered and thudded again and then became still. The driver climbed out, straightened his checked cloth cap, and went to the side of the van to open the wide doors. He started to pull out the ramp and the man in the back swung out of the van to help. He was a big man, with wide shoulders, and the lights which were on in the van shot bright highlights onto his fair hair.

The two men settled the ramp into place and fitted the wings on each side of the ramp with care. The horse inside started pawing and the big man spoke to him in a low voice.

Finally the wings were fixed in place to their satisfaction. The big man disappeared into the van. Crumb was getting restless; he fidgeted a little and for an awful moment I thought he was going to whinny. I slipped quickly off his back and put my hand on his muzzle, just above his nostrils, ready to clamp down on him if he started to make any noise. I'd read about this trick in a book on Indians in school and I hoped the author knew what he was talking about, because I had a very strong feeling that these two men, whoever they were, would not be pleased to know they had an audience.

There was a sagging old hay barn on the edge of the field that hadn't been used for years. It made me jump when lights suddenly went on inside it. At the same time the silhouette of a big horse, blanketed and with his legs wrapped in protective shipping bandages, appeared at the door to the van. There was a quick rush of hoofbeats as the horse skittered down the ramp and danced briefly at the end of the lead shank before putting his head down to snatch at the grass in the field.

Crumb grew tense and started to open his mouth, as I had been dreading he would. But I hung onto him, trying to let him breathe without giving him the chance to make any sound. He quieted down again while I watched and waited.

A few minutes later the lights were switched off, the two men shut the door of the old barn, slid the ramp up, and took off in the van.

I heard the horse whinny once, kind of sadly, as though he understood they were leaving him alone.

This time, Indians or no Indians, I couldn't stop The Crumb—maybe I was just sorry for the horse in the dark shed, all by himself miles from home—anyway, Crumb answered, just once, and then everything was quiet again.

Stars were coming out. Mother would be having a fit if I didn't get home pretty soon. I led my pony over to the barn, wondering if I dared open the door and switch on the lights, just for a second, to look at the horse—but there was no chance. The doors were padlocked.

The Crumb and I just stood there, feeling frustrated and foolish—at least I did, I really can't speak for The Crumb—so finally I did the only sensible thing I could think of. I climbed onto The Crumb and went home.

## Chapter 2

Mom was furious, of course, so I washed my hair without any argument and brushed it dry while I finished my homework, and managed to get to bed on time. This pacified Mom, kept my older brother

Tim off my back, and got me into bed where I lay and stared out the window practically all night, wondering about the barn.

Even Miss Pritchard, my teacher, worried about me the next day, and said I looked pale and asked if I had any problems I'd like to talk to her about. I was terribly polite—my father is principal of the school, which can be quite a burden sometimes, believe me—so I murmured something about cramps. Miss Pritchard patted me tenderly on the shoulder and suddenly I found myself excused from school and sent home early.

It took me all of two seconds to yank on my jeans and jacket and set out for the hills on The Crumb. It was a lot colder than it had been the day before. The wind was damp and clammy and blew the pony's tail in all directions, which he hated, and he actually managed to dump me off by bucking through an open gate. I was insulted, the pony was cross, and we were barely communicating by the time we got to the back woods again. Fortunately, the wind stayed in the tops of the trees and the paths were quiet and warmer, and The Crumb and I had reached a better understanding by the time we got back to the old hay barn.

I got off the pony and led him to the edge of the woods, very slowly, just in case, but there was no one there. The horse was still inside the barn. He whinnied at Crumb and Crumb whinnied back—but there were no people, only some fresh tire tracks over the tracks left by the van the night before. The doors were padlocked shut. The padlock was strong and new, and so were the metal latches on the door. I didn't go too close—I didn't want Crumb to leave hoofprints in the soft ground near the barn—because I was absolutely sure something really strange was happening here and the last thing I wanted was to be found snooping around.

I rode home again and made myself a cup of tea to keep up the pretended invalid image, curled up on the sofa with a book, and fell asleep. I would have liked to talk to somebody about what I'd seen, but when Mom came home and found me sleeping, she was wild—she's a worrier—so I had to make a terrific effort to be bright and cheerful, which wore me out completely. I slept like a log and looked like new the next morning.

This kept me in school all day, of course, but the weather was glorious and I got on The Crumb as soon as I could after I got home. We had a wonderful ride, chasing the wind and the cloud shadows around the pastures and jumping the barways and the stone walls—Mr. Martin, the farmer, isn't too young any more, and he doesn't keep his fences built up very well, which was nice for The Crumb and me as there were always parts of the walls fallen low enough for us to jump.

But when we got near the back pasture we both settled down. I had left the pony's halter on under his bridle and knotted a lead rope around his neck, so I was able to tie him safely in the woods and sneak out to the hay barn on foot. But again there was nothing to see. Just more fresh tire tracks, a few wisps of hay, and a few footprints in the mud near the door. Even the horse inside—if there was still a horse inside—was quiet, though I thought I heard him sneeze softly, just once.

By this time I was hardly worried any more. I was almost out of my mind with curiosity instead. I even wondered whether or not to tell my brother about it, which shows how desperate I must have been, because he would have immediately leaped onto his motorcycle and roared over there with as much secrecy as a Fourth of July parade. Luckily, I still had enough brains to keep quiet, because the next afternoon, when I went back to look, the barn was empty.

I couldn't tell at first, of course. I went through the whole scene of tying up the pony and tiptoeing furtively through the woods, only to find myself looking foolishly at the unlocked doors, which had been left slightly open.

I eased through the gap and went into the barn. It still had the warm smell of live horses. There was a small pile of hay and some bedding in one corner. There was one box stall, with a few new boards obviously replacing others that had been worn or broken, and there was a damp mark on the wall where a water bucket had been fastened.

I stood in the middle of the stall, brooding. I had a let-down, cheated feeling, because I felt now I'd never know what this had all been about.

The sunlight was slanting through the door and it lit the cracks between the wide planks of the floor, and that's how I saw the hypodermic syringe sparkle. It wasn't the syringe itself that sparkled, of course, because it was one of those disposable ones made of plastic, but the metal on the tip caught the sunlight where the needle had been broken off. I fished it up from between the planks where it was lying, using a stick I found just outside the door. There was a scrap of cotton jammed between the boards, too, and I pried it out. It had dried, dark-brown stains on it that could have been either iodine or blood—I couldn't tell which. I found shreds of bandage in the discarded bedding, and then I searched for another few minutes but couldn't find anything more that was even vaguely interesting.

I felt sure this was all very significant, but I couldn't

imagine what it meant. I had a tattered piece of Kleenex in my pants pocket, so I wrapped the syringe and the cotton together and put them in the pocket of my jacket. I took a last look around, then ran back to where The Crumb was waiting impatiently, having eaten all the buds off the branches he could reach on the tree where I'd left him tied.

The Crumb lived in a lovely big box stall built onto the side of our garage by my father and my brother Tim, who had growled and snapped through the whole building procedure and then bragged when it was done as though it was the Taj Mahal and he'd built it himself. We didn't have much land, but Mr. Martin's farm was right beside us, so we had a small paddock on our own place, and in good weather The Crumb shared Mr. Martin's big field with the cows.

I spent extra time putting the pony away, fed him, and generally tucked him in for the night, before going into the house. Tim was in the kitchen, foraging in the refrigerator as though he were starving.

The casserole in the oven was giving off heavenly smells, and I was hungry, and I just plain wasn't thinking when I turned out my pockets onto the kitchen table looking for a favorite pen that had worked its way through a tiny hole into the lining of my jacket.

It wasn't until I heard Tim make the most ghastly choking sound that I realized what I'd done. The hypodermic syringe and the stained piece of cotton had come unwrapped and were lying there in plain sight, along with a quarter, two safety pins, a half-consumed chocolate bar, and the fugitive pen I'd been looking for.

"Cindy!" said Tim and turned white as a sheet—he really did, just as people are always doing in romantic novels. I thought he was going to faint dead away, like the time he broke his arm playing football.

"Don't jump to stupid conclusions," I said, as calmly as possible under the circumstances.

I started to put the stuff back in my pocket, but before I had the chance Tim had swooped over and picked up the syringe. "What's in this thing?" he said.

"I don't know." I tried to look unconcerned and even a little bored. Tim held the syringe up to the light, as though this would answer all his questions—he had so many he didn't know how to start asking them all.

"Where'd you get it?" he asked finally.

"Found it."

"Found it *where*?"

"In a barn."

"In a *barn*? What kind of barns do you go to on those rides of yours?"

"Just an old barn, an old hay barn, and whatever

it is you're thinking, you can just quit, Timothy Blake." I was starting to get mad. I was working at it, of course. I knew my face was red enough, anyway. I was furious at myself for being so stupid as to drag that thing out into plain sight, and I figured I would switch it all around to make my fury look like righteous indignation.

Tim gave me a funny look and marched out of the kitchen. "Where are you going?" I said, running after him. "That thing may be evidence!" I was feeling very dramatic.

"Evidence!" Tim snorted. He snatched his jacket off the coat hook by the back door and stomped outside, slamming the door behind him. Then he opened the door again and stuck his head back inside. "This kind of evidence, as you call it, isn't exactly what Mom needs to find lying around in your room, stupid. Or Dad either. He'll be home any minute. I'm going to get rid of this thing, and then you're going to tell me what this is all about."

He slammed the door again, hard enough to crack the glass, only it didn't crack, which was too bad, because it would have served him right.

# Chapter 3

I refused to discuss it with him. He threatened, he bribed, and he coaxed, but I had told him the truth about the syringe and I wouldn't tell him anything more. Poor Tim. I guess I was pretty hard on him, and he was really concerned, but I didn't care. Eventually he stopped trying and went on with his own life and left me pretty much alone, though I used to catch him watching me occasionally.

I had other problems to worry about. My financial situation was reaching the point of sheer disaster. Spring had truly come and I was grateful beyond belief, because The Crumb had rolled once too often in his heavy winter blanket and it had popped its seams and was full of holes. It was worn out. This meant that I absolutely had to replace it by next fall—and though I didn't want to admit it to myself, the pony was getting too old to go through another winter without two heavy blankets, no matter how thick a coat he grew, and winter blankets were horribly expensive. The money I made baby-sitting and helping out at occasional birthday parties barely covered his routine feeding and shoeing, but extras such as expensive blankets were way out of reach.

I still wondered now and then about the mysterious horse in the deserted barn, especially at dusk when the light changed and I remembered with a shiver how strange the van had looked coming across the empty field. But wondering brought no answers, and there were other things to occupy me—incidentals like school work and important things like The Crumb's catching an awful cold and coughing and sneezing and running a fever. The vet came three times to give him shots and powdered medicines, which he wouldn't eat in his grain, which meant he had to have more shots. Then I had to borrow money from Mom to pay the vet bills, which I hated to do, and The Crumb and I had to miss the first local spring show because he'd been so sick, and everything was a complete mess in all directions.

Once his cough and fever had gone, I was able to ride The Crumb slowly and gently, and we ambled over the fields together and went by the old barn one morning. There was nothing left to tell of its mysterious occupant other than the bright metal of the newer latches on the doors, and even they were beginning to weather slowly and lose their shine. Grass and weeds had grown up over the deep tire tracks left by the van. Spring rains had just about leveled them anyway.

A girl I didn't like very much came by on her

horse one Saturday morning and gave me an idea
that changed a lot of things. I was pulling The
Crumb's mane, making it short and smooth, and
it really did look nice, even though I say so myself.
Ann waited until I'd finished and turned The Crumb
out into his paddock.

"You sure can do a terrific job on a pony," she
said with real admiration as The Crumb trotted
away from the gate. "That pony of yours always
looks as nice as those fancy ones over at the Ashford
place." Coming from her, that remark was extra-
ordinary, and I was grateful all out of proportion
and even managed to find some nice things to say
about her horse. Ann waved and rode off down the
road.

I stood and watched her go, and the idea she had
given me took root and grew like crazy. I went into
the house, found a pair of sneakers without too many
holes, put on a fresh shirt, tied my hair back, and
went to get a job.

Just across the ridge from us was the stable Ann
had mentioned. It was immaculately kept. There
was never a fence rail out of place, the rings and
paddocks looked like lawns, there were flower beds
beside the driveway in the front and two rings and
a jumping course in the fields in the back.

All of this belonged to Jan Ashford, who owned two or three nice young Thoroughbreds and a promising young show jumper, but most of one long wing of her place was filled with show ponies. She boarded them, schooled them and taught their owners, took them to shows, and was slowly making her quiet presence felt in the big shows in our area.

Our paths seldom crossed. Crumb and I were perfectly content to go to the one-day, smaller shows nearby. Every once in a while I'd see Jan out riding on the bridle paths either alone or with a few of her pupils on their ponies. Sometimes she'd bring a young pony or a nervous new owner to a small show for experience. The ponies in her charge were usually so beautiful that they made the rest of us, with our backyard ponies, feel a little foolish. Jan understood and she didn't do this very often.

I'd been at our town library the evening Jan showed movies of our Equestrian Team at the last Olympics. Several of my friends and I stayed on afterward to talk to her—she actually knew some of the riders—and she answered our questions with terrific patience. She'd been in London when our team won the *Horse and Hound* Cup; she'd been in Rome when we didn't win at all. She described the courses in Europe and the horses that jumped them, and when we finally left the library hours later, our heads were reeling with the excitement of it all, and Crumb and I jumped triple bars and rail-and-ditch arrangements in the cow pasture for weeks afterward.

Jan asked us to come to see her stable, which all of us did at one time or another, but we felt a little shy about intruding, I guess, because we didn't go over very often. At least, I certainly didn't, but on this particular day I leaped onto my bicycle (a lot of people don't like strange horses coming to their stables, so I didn't take Crumb) and rode over to her place before I could give myself the chance to change my mind.

The place was a madhouse. Quietly so, but a madhouse, just the same. Parents sat in their station wagons and chatted or read, some of the mothers were doing needlepoint, and they all looked very calm, but inside the stable there were ponies and little girls looking frantic and Jan, by herself, trying to find someone's crop and someone else's bridle, while trying to get the children onto their ponies and into the ring for a lesson.

I couldn't possibly have come at a more fortunate time for me. With hardly a word, I went to work. Other than putting a dark-haired child with braids onto a pony that belonged to someone else, I swooped and coped well in fifty different directions. I shortened stirrups, straightened curb chains, and generally made myself so useful that the ponies were sorted out, in the ring, and trotting about with their riders before they knew what hit them. Gasping a little, I draped myself over the rail and beamed at the ring full of ponies. I had the comfortable feeling that I had a job before I'd even asked for one.

Jan gave me a grateful wave and started teaching right away. We didn't have the chance to speak another word until the lesson was over, the ponies were cool and safely back in their stalls, the last black hunt cap had been found and sent off with its small owner, and the last car had vanished down the drive.

"Hello," Jan said at last. "You're Cindy Blake, aren't you, with that nice dun pony that jumps so well? I remember—you came over to see my place once, but that was several months ago." She led the way along the spotless aisle between the stalls to her office near the tack room, and she sat down wearily on the couch.

"I don't know what I would have done without you this morning," she said. "All the children seem to want to ride at the same time, and neither of the stable boys came in this morning even to help tack up the ponies. It's really more than I can manage. You wouldn't like to make this a regular thing, would you? I'd pay you, of course."

"I'd like to, very much," I said.

"I know you're still in school," Jan said with a

smile. "But so are almost all of the riders, so they ride mostly on weekends and I turn their ponies out in the paddocks to exercise on days they can't be ridden. Weekdays are no problem. But weekends!" She shook her head and tucked a stray wisp of hair back into place. The phone rang and Jan turned to answer it. I made a quick, dazed promise to return the next morning, leaped onto my bicycle, and rattled happily down the long drive.

As I got near the main road, I heard the growl of changing gears and the hiss of brakes, and a large horse van turned through the brick pillars at the entrance to the drive. I hopped off the bike and moved out of the way to let it go by, and as I stood there by the rail fence, you can imagine how I felt when I saw the driver was wearing a checked cap. The van was cherry red, with "Ashford Farms" lettered in white beside the door—I was close enough, this time, to read the name. And sitting next to the driver was the big, blond man I'd seen that night in the field.

I waited and I watched it go by like a ghost from a half-forgotten bad dream. There was just one horse in the van—I could see nothing more than its head through the top open window—but it was a gray horse and so could not possibly have been the mystery horse I'd seen that strange evening. Though it had been too dark to tell what other color that horse had been, whatever it was, it hadn't been gray.

So I stood in the grass and wondered vaguely about the possibility of poison ivy near the fence, and my brain felt like a scrambled egg. It was almost impossible for me to imagine that Jan Ashford could, in any way, be mixed up in anything as weird as that scene in the cow pasture, but these were the two men I'd seen in the field that night, and they certainly had been driving the Ashford van.

## Chapter 4

I went home as puzzled and uncertain as I'd ever been in my life. I didn't want any lunch, so I went straight out to get The Crumb. He was capering around in the cow pasture with his tail in the air, looking like an idiot, while the cows surveyed him tranquilly. He was awful to catch, which isn't usually a problem with him. I think I'd spoiled him a little while he was sick. I finally had to go and get some oats and I rattled them in the bottom of a bucket until he couldn't stand it any longer. He came over to grab a mouthful of grain and became my prisoner.

He accepted his capture philosophically and we were soon out in the fields together. I tried to gather my wandering wits and make some sense of what I knew.

The trouble was that I didn't really know anything, other than that I'd seen the Ashford van before, in a strange place and at a strange time of day. But what did that mean? What difference could it make to me, anyway? There was nothing illegal about putting a horse in a barn, after all. As for the syringe I'd found, it could have been there for a thousand different reasons, all of them perfectly innocent. I'd counted, and the vet had used seven disposable syringes in the few days The Crumb had been sick.

So I fussed and worried a little bit more, and The Crumb grew bored and began grinding his teeth on the bit for something to do as we wandered along. I hated it when he did this, which he knew very well, so I gave him a cross kick in the ribs, he put his ears back and looked sour, and we dragged our way home.

Mom was outside weeding and raking the dead leaves out of one of the garden beds. She said I looked like the last rose of summer. I thought this was an appropriate remark for a change, because I did feel prickly all over.

But I smiled and said everything was wonderful.

Mom patted The Crumb a little uncertainly. She wasn't too crazy about horses, but she believed riding was terrifically healthy, unless I wasn't home by dark. Then she was always sure that both the pony and I were dead in a ditch somewhere. I don't know why she never thought I might fall off in broad daylight and slowly bleed to death while Crumb stuffed his face with grass nearby. Maybe she thought he'd run home, snorting and neighing for help like the horses in television programs. I don't know; I've certainly never discussed this with her. If this is what she thought, I'd hate to be the one to tell her this isn't the way things work in real life.

Anyway, The Crumb put on his sappy look, so Mom went to get him a carrot. I don't like him to eat with his bit in his mouth, but I didn't want to discourage Mom. Crumb managed quite well while I groaned to myself over the little scraps of carrot he was getting all over his bit and his reins.

As soon as I possibly could I put him away in his stall and cleaned the bit and bridle. It wasn't until dinner that night that I finally cheered up and told the whole family about my new job for the summer. They were all very pleased for me. By the time I went to bed I was feeling a lot better. My financial situation would soon be in great shape. I would probably be able to afford a new light summer sheet for The Crumb to match the new blankets I was going to get for him, and I finally fell asleep.

I helped with the ponies and the children's lessons the next day. When we were done, Jan and I went into the office to arrange the lessons for the next weekend, and while we were there the office door opened and the big, blond man I'd seen with the van came in.

"Cindy, have you met Alex?" said Jan. "Cindy Blake, this is Alex Russell. You may never have met, Cindy, but I'm sure you've seen Alex ride."

I murmured all the polite things I was supposed to and hoped my smile looked more real than it felt. Alex just nodded and turned to Jan. "I need the van again this morning," he said. "I'm going to pick up that four-year-old mare at the McKays' place."

Jan looked surprised. "You mean Bright Interval? That nice chestnut mare Larry's been schooling and showing?"

Alex grinned as Jan handed him a set of keys. "Larry hasn't been winning as much as the owners would like," he said, tossing the keys and then putting them in his pocket. "They want me to see what I can do."

They went on talking and even though the talk was about horses, I didn't listen. Alex Russell. Of course I'd seen him ride. Though The Crumb and I didn't go to the big horse shows together, I went to watch whenever I could, and Alex Russell was always there. What I couldn't understand was what he was doing *here*, in Jan's office, borrowing her van, as though he belonged. Any more than I could understand what he'd been doing unloading a horse in the half-dark of a deserted cow pasture.

I said nothing, of course. Alex left, Jan was in a hurry, and there was no time to ask questions. I wouldn't have known what kind of questions to ask anyway.

The next Saturday morning it started to rain just after I reached the stable. The wind rose and lashed the rain against the windows and all the morning classes were cancelled. Jan and I made cocoa on the small stove in the tack room and sat with steaming mugs watching the trees beside the ring whipping their branches in the wind. It was cozy and warm in the tack room and we chatted lazily about the ponies and the summer shows to come.

"I think it's all going to work out," Jan said. "I wasn't sure at first, but I'm glad I came back here to give it a try. This place, Ashford Farms, used to belong to my father, years ago. He bred and showed a few nice horses and kept his hunters here. When he died, he left it all to me. I didn't pay much attention to it for a while. I had a good job and I did a lot of traveling, so I sold all the horses and closed the place up.

"But I missed the horses more than I'd thought I would. I started riding again whenever I could. I like teaching and I like working with children, so I took a year's leave of absence from my job to see if I could manage on my own.

"I didn't want to start out by taking on too much too soon, so I just opened half the stable and took a few pupils and their ponies. I've found I like it very much, and I want to go on with it."

She got up and poured fresh cocoa into our mugs, stopped to frown at the driving rain, and came back and sat down.

"There's a lot more room here to expand, and I'll do it as soon as I can, but I'll have to wait until Alex moves out." Jan made a face. "I thought he was going to be here only a few weeks, but I did feel sorry for him—did you know his own place burned down last fall?"

I shook my head silently. I didn't want to interrupt by saying anything out loud. I didn't want to distract her, not when she was about to tell me, finally, what Alex was doing at her place.

"It was a terrible fire. It started late at night. Alex

was away; Dan, who helped run the stable, was living in a house nearby, but he was asleep. A truck driver saw the flames from the road and reported the fire and then got to the stable as quickly as he could. He didn't know very much about horses, but he was able to get three of them out. It was a tragic loss—almost thirty horses died, most of them riding school horses; Alex was just trying to get started with a few show jumpers, which weren't amounting to much, but he did have one good horse. And it was just the most fantastic luck that in all that awful smoke and fire, one of the horses the truck driver managed to get out was Cat Burglar."

I nodded. I knew the horse. So did everyone everywhere who was interested in show jumping. I'd seen the horse jump at a show last summer when he won a huge class, beating five of the horses that were on their way to Europe with our Equestrian Team. He was a tall, leggy brown horse and he was perfectly named—he moved the way you'd imagine a cat burglar would move—silently and smoothly, slipping over his fences like a shadow.

Jan laughed quietly. "Alex and Cat certainly rocked a lot of boats last year," she said. "It's a shock when a horse like that comes out of nowhere and wins the way he did. I think he was just as big a surprise to Alex. He's been in the game a long time and he's never had a horse of that much ability before.

"Anyway, Cat Burglar survived and all the professional horsemen in our area got together to help Alex out. He'd lost everything—tack and vans and trailers. I told him he could bring his horses here until he could get started again." Jan sighed. "To be honest, I expected him to be here only a short time, and with just a few horses, but ever since he's been making such a name for himself winning with Cat, he keeps getting new clients and the whole other wing of my place is filling up now. They keep pretty much to themselves, but I sure could use the room."

Jan stood up, stretched, and went over to the window. "I've got enough extra stalls for the rest of this season anyway," she said. "Just look at that rain! It's days like this that make me wish I had an indoor ring. Maybe I'll have to start thinking about putting one up in a year or so, if things go well."

We talked about this possibility, and where the ring might be built, and Jan finally took me home in her car because the rain showed no signs of letting up.

Even without riding, it had been a good morning. I was content. As I'd found out a lot of times before this, if I kept my mouth shut and listened, I eventually discovered what I wanted to know. Whatever had been going on in Mr. Martin's old barn, the chances were it was all Alex's doing, and Jan probably knew nothing about it.

# Chapter 5

**S**pring vacation started and I spent most of my time with Jan. The early show season was about to begin and there was a lot to do. Every saddle and bridle had to be checked over and a single frayed stitch or the least trace of wear was enough to mark for repair or replacement. Shipping bandages were washed and dried and rerolled for each pony. Blankets, fly sheets and waterproof rain sheets and woolen coolers were shaken out, cleaned if necessary, and refolded into each pony's own tack trunk.

We pulled manes, trimmed tails and fetlocks, clipped muzzles and ears, and schooled and worked over each pony as though it were the only one in the stable. There were seven of them when we started (though it had seemed as though there'd been a couple of dozen that first confused afternoon), and it was great fun working with them and getting to know them as individuals.

Some were sweet and some were holy terrors. The worst was a glorious chestnut mare who stood like an angel for everything we did until it was time to trim her ears. Then she fought like a wildcat. Even when we used the tiny silent clipping machine, she struck out with her forelegs and flung herself around in a frenzy. We tried stuffing cotton in her ears, we asked two of Alex's grooms to help, and finally we had to call the vet to zap her with enough tranquilizers to put an elephant out for a week. It took all of five minutes to do her ears, eight hours for the tranquilizers to wear off, and a month before I could look at her without wanting to strangle her with my bare hands.

Jan accepted the whole battle with serenity. "Almost every horse or pony ever foaled has got a hang-up of one kind or another," she said. "Ponies and horses aren't pets, and you can't expect them to be. Good show ponies have a job to do, and when they can do it well, you learn to cope. They're worth the trouble."

I watched, and I listened, and I learned. I had my favorites, of course (the chestnut mare wasn't one of them). I particularly liked a small gray Welsh pony with tiny ears and a lovely head. He had a Welsh name nobody could pronounce, so we called him Sam. He belonged to a little girl named Angie, with long, dark pigtails, and the two of them together would have jumped the moon if they'd been asked. Jan and I were forever rushing out to discourage them from trying the huge jumps set up for the big horses on the outside course.

Another of my favorites was a beautiful red-bay

mare they called Whispering Sands. She was only four years old and my insides turned to a mush of longing to ride her whenever I saw her. She was slim and elegant, sired by an Arabian out of a Connemara mare, and she was as inexperienced and green as spring grass. Her owner couldn't be bothered to ride her when the weather wasn't absolutely perfect, or lots of other times when riding just wasn't convenient, so Jan usually rode and schooled her until one wonderful morning she put me up on her and told me to join the others practicing in the ring.

I felt I'd died and gone to heaven that day. The mare moved like silk; I could hardly feel her feet touch the ground. Jan was a stern and demanding teacher and I don't think I made a move she didn't see, correct, and have me do again. I loved every minute of it.

Sometimes we took a morning off and went to look at ponies for new clients. One of the biggest problems was trying to find a pony for Gregory, who had red hair and freckles and who was the little brother of the girl who owned Sam.

Gregory wanted a pony of his own more than anything in the world and we had an awful time trying to find him one. We went to look at them, we brought many of them back to try for him, and Jan asked everyone she knew to keep an eye out for a small pony for a child. You'd have thought we were looking for a diamond in a desert—there didn't seem to be any small ponies *anywhere* you could trust with a beginner.

It seemed to me we tried a hundred, but I suppose there were really no more than twenty, and we sent all of them back where they came from. They bit or kicked or ran away, and there was one sweet little palomino both of us liked at first. We thought we'd finally found Greg his pony, and one day in the ring while I was riding him to try him out, I turned to Jan to comment on how well the pony was going.

The next thing I knew he'd flung himself down on the ground and was trying to roll on me.

"Good ponies are hard to find," said Jan as she dusted me off and we put the pony away in disgrace. I was so mad I could hardly speak. My leg hurt where I'd hit it on a rock, my shoulder was stiff, and I had half the ring dirt down the back of my neck and in my hair. At least it felt that way. I don't mind going off occasionally, but it was embarrassing to have been outwitted by a small, fat pony who had such a sweet look and the manners of the devil.

Eventually, a friend of our blacksmith appeared in the stable yard in a Volkswagen bus. "Hear you're looking for a kid's pony," he said. He opened the doors and a little black and white pony jumped out.

This one stayed. His name was Skipper and he was perfect. Greg rode him everywhere and Jan and I thankfully turned our attention back to our other duties.

Poor Crumb was sadly neglected all these weeks. I kept him as well and fit as I always had, but my time was short and my rides on him were duty rides to exercise him instead of the fun wanderings we'd done so much before. Then Jan asked about him one day and suggested I ride him over to the stable instead of using that miserable bicycle. And because he was so steady and sensible, I started riding in front to lead the way when the little riders went out on their ponies on the bridle paths, while Jan brought up the rear to scoop up any fallen bodies along the way.

I don't know how she had the patience. Very often the ponies behaved like brats, or their riders did, weeping and wailing and dropping their crops or losing their hunt caps every two minutes.

New ponies came as the show season grew closer. Jan kept casting longing looks at the second wing of her stable still being used by Alex, but he showed no signs of moving out. I'd gone over once or twice to look at his horses, and admired them cautiously from outside their stalls, but neither Alex nor Dan, his head groom, seemed the least bit pleased to have me, so I soon gave up and stayed away.

I watched Alex working with his horses (from a distance) whenever I could. Since he usually exercised them early in the mornings, I didn't see him often, but I was surprised to find out that he wasn't really such a good rider, especially on the young Thoroughbred show hunters he was getting ready for his clients. The whole thing seemed to me a case of a second-rate horseman on first-rate horses, but certainly I was no expert, and Alex had a fabulous reputation of winning on Cat Burglar and this brought clients to him in droves.

We were kept so busy that there wasn't much time to watch Alex anyway. Some of the pony owners were terrific; they were dedicated and skillful and worked under Jan with an intensity that was wonderful to watch. Others couldn't have cared less, like the girl who owned Whispering Sands. And there was another, a new client, with a superb gray pony, who wouldn't listen to a word Jan said.

She nagged her pony, whacking him with her crop and jabbing him in the mouth with the reins every time he did the least little thing that displeased her. Jan pleaded with her, coaxed her, and then one day even lost her temper and shouted at her, but it made no difference.

Of course it all ended in disaster; this pony was well bred, well fed, and driven to desperation. He took off with his rider one bright morning and smashed through the ring fence. There was a great wreck, with the pony turning over in a heap. He ripped a gash in his chest and his rider hurt her shoulder, and you'd have thought the world was coming to an end. There were screaming sirens and ambulances and shrieks and moans from the rider and her mother—all the adults rushed to the rescue. I led the poor pony back to the stable and sent for the vet.

Jan came storming in a few minutes later, shaking with rage (I'd never seen her upset like this before), and when she'd calmed down a little she reported that the mother was insisting that this dangerous pony be shot.

Fortunately the mother had gone off with her poor dear suffering child in the ambulance, which gave me time to calm Jan down a little before the vet came. But then he arrived in a fury, too. It seemed that the mother had called his answering service and ordered the pony destroyed. So with a tact I didn't know I had, I got them both calmed down, and the vet stitched the pony's cut gently and ordered cold compresses for its swollen knee. He drove off swearing he'd shoot himself first before he'd put that good pony down.

# Chapter 6

**W**hat with this and that, it was a very busy time. Jan and the vet managed somehow to get the hurt pony sent away somewhere, the injured rider turned out to have nothing more than a tiny crack in her collarbone, and in a few weeks the whole thing blew over. The pony was sold. The girl who'd owned him gave up riding because she said she'd been so shattered by her ghastly experience, and took up tennis instead—I heard her saying this one morning when she came to pick up a sweater she'd left at the stables—and we didn't miss her at all.

School ended at last and the show season opened with a bang. Jan and I went to the first show with four of the ponies. Sam, the Welsh pony, covered himself with glory and won every small pony class in the show. The streamers of his championship ribbon reached almost to his knees. I found his small rider behind the van at the end of the day, sobbing with joy with her arms around her pony's neck, and her mother told me, a few days later, that the child had slept with the ribbon that night, along with a snapshot of her beloved pony.

The others didn't do quite so well, but they did

well enough, winning their share of ribbons. Whispering Sands was confused by all the excitement but was a credit to her owner (and to me, too—after all, I'd done most of her schooling), and as Jan and I undid the braided manes and tails when we got the ponies back home that night, we agreed wearily but happily that it had been a promising beginning for the season ahead.

It was hard work, but I liked it all. There was always so much to do. The day before the show, we braided the ponies, washed the gray ones and the white markings on the dark ones, checked the contents of each tack trunk, and generally got the ponies and their belongings in order. I even liked the dark early mornings when Jan would come by the house to pick me up and we would drive to the stables together to help load the ponies into the van and see them off. We would follow in Jan's station wagon and get to the show grounds well before the show started—Jan hated to hustle the ponies before their first class and tried to be strict about the riders getting to the show on time.

Sometimes we took some of the riders with us and that was fun, listening to them chatter about their ponies. Sometimes one of them would be nervous and quiet, and it was funny how some of the best riders would get pale and shaky right up to the first class, but I was full of sympathy because I'd felt that way, too, even at the smaller shows with Crumb.

When we got to the show grounds, we all helped to polish the ponies, put their riders up, and send them off to warm up. Either Jan or I had to supervise the younger ones, because once they were out of sight they were tempted to race their ponies around and wear them out before the first class even started.

The older riders were less inclined to overdo. Actually some of them could hardly be bothered to warm up their ponies or give them a school over the course, so I would do this for them if they didn't show up on time. Much as I had to pretend to be shocked by their behavior, I secretly looked forward to the days this happened. I loved riding these good ponies for any reason, and once I even had the chance to ride Whispering Sands in a hack class and win it, before her rider bothered to show up.

Jan was pleased. The owner was slightly annoyed because the mare had gone so well for me, but the silver bowl she got with the blue ribbon made her happy, even though she hadn't won it herself.

Sam, the Welsh pony, stepped on a stone and bruised his foot badly. Angie sat in his stall at Jan's and read books to him by the hour while he stood with his foot wrapped in wet dressings. The pony seemed to enjoy all the fuss; I know Angie did.

In a few days he was able to hobble around in the paddock with a neat plastic boot strapped to his hoof to protect it, and eventually he stopped limping. The vet said he'd have to wear shoes for several weeks, with leather pads between the shoe and the hoof, to prevent any more bruising. Sam had often had his feet trimmed by the blacksmith, but, like many small ponies, his hoofs were so tough he usually did not need to wear shoes.

The blacksmith came, fitted the first shoe, and started to nail it on. At the first tap of the hammer Sam exploded like a firecracker—there were practically sparks coming out of his ears. There was no reason for it, he hadn't been hurt, but Sam didn't like the tapping and he was determined not to let the blacksmith do any more.

Sam fought stubbornly while Jan and I hung on to him, just as determined as he was. Eventually, with the added help of the blacksmith's assistant and the driver of the feed truck who'd come to deliver some hay, we were able to hold the pony still long enough for the blacksmith to set both front shoes in place.

Gasping for breath, I trotted the pony out. The blacksmith watched, nodded, and grinned wearily at Jan. "Those little devils can be worse to shoe than a hurricane," he said. "It's a good thing this pony doesn't need shoeing on his hind feet, too, or I'd have to take a week's vacation to recover."

I turned Sam into the paddock and he trotted away from the gate, tossing his head and prancing as though he'd won the whole battle. We all stood by the paddock fence, still a little out of breath, and then Jan suddenly grabbed my arm.

"Catch him, quick!" she said. "I've just had the most awful thought!" She ran back toward the stable.

I couldn't imagine what was wrong, but I hurried to do what I'd been told and trotted the surprised pony back to the stable yard.

"He's got shoes on now!" said Jan.

"I know he does. I was there," I said, rubbing a stiff shoulder. I looked at the pony's round little forehoofs and knelt to feel them for any signs of inflammation. "No heat, they're fine," I told Jan.

"Just hold him still," said Jan. I looked at Sam's sweet expression a little more thoughtfully than I usually did. Holding Sam still obviously wasn't always a simple thing to do. I braced myself as Jan quietly brought a measuring stick from behind her back and moved toward the plump gray pony.

Sam did no more than snort a few times and roll his dark eyes, then he stood like a rock while Jan put the tall stick next to his shoulder and moved the crosspiece down until it reached the top of his withers.

"Can you see the bubble in the level in the cross-piece?" asked Jan. I peered over her shoulder.

"Right in the middle," I said.

"Okay," said Jan. "Now you do it." She took the pony's lead rope from my hand and gave me the stick.

I measured carefully and squinted at the markings on the stick. "Twelve hands, one and one-half inches," I said. "Forty-nine and a half inches altogether."

"That's what I got," said Jan with a relieved sigh. "You sure you've got the crosspiece absolutely level?"

"Bubble's in the middle," I said patiently.

"Right. You can turn him out again." Jan went to the tack room with the measuring stick. I put the pony out into the paddock again and then went and found Jan in her office with Sam's file folder in her hand.

"Remind me," said Jan. "Sam should be officially re-measured the next time he's shown. He's got a permanent measurement card, but he was measured without shoes, so he ought to get a new one." She clipped a note to the top of the file and put it back in the drawer. "I was worried half to death," she said. "I was afraid he'd be over twelve and a half hands now he has shoes on, and that would have put him right out of the small pony division. He could have jumped the bigger fences without any trouble, but Angie isn't ready. Those few more inches can make a big difference to an inexperienced youngster."

At Sam's next show I took him to be measured for his new card. There was one pony already waiting, a tall, showy golden chestnut with four white stockings and blaze. The girl who was holding him looked nervous and she gave an enormous smile of relief when a man in glistening black boots and a smart riding coat came to take the pony's lead rope from her hand.

I recognized him; he'd been at almost every show we'd been to this summer. His name was Roger Hill, and he had a string of clients that seemed to grow at every show. His ponies were all elegant and beautiful and impeccably turned out. So were the children who rode them. He scared me a little, to be honest, because he was ferocious when one of the riders made a mistake, or one of the ponies misbehaved, though this didn't happen very often.

Roger smiled at the officials as they came over. He led the pony onto the level concrete measuring surface. The pony, who had been standing calmly, began to sweat and fidget uneasily and when the measuring stick was brought near him, I thought the poor thing was going to throw himself down on the ground. There was a sort of a flurry, the pony held still for a second, and then Roger thanked the officials quickly and led the pony away.

"What on earth's the matter with your pony?" I said to the girl who was waiting tensely nearby.

"Shut up," she said. So I did. Sam was next. He stood quietly to be measured and was pronounced to be safely under the height limit for small ponies. I hurried him back to the van and gave Jan Sam's new measurement certificate. And the first chance I got, I described how the chestnut pony had acted.

Jan made a face. "Bet that was one of Roger Hill's," she said. I nodded. "Very breedy pony, lots of quality? Four white stockings and a blaze?" I nodded again.

Jan shrugged her shoulders disgustedly. "That thing's no pony," she said. "That's a small horse, or I'll eat it with a spoon. I went to look at it last summer for clients who were interested in a show pony for their son. The breeder said it was a five-year-old, but it looked to me more like four. Whatever it was, it still had some growing to do, and I felt it would go over the pony height limit, so I turned it down. I heard Roger'd bought it a few weeks later."

"But it passed," I said. "It's in the pony division. The steward said it was fourteen-two. I heard him tell Roger."

Jan laughed, but she didn't sound very amused. "You bet it passed. If you put a squeaky one like that into Roger's hands, it'll pass. He schools it a few times with a tack in the measuring stick, so the crossbar pricks the pony when the bar is brought down near its withers. The pony soon learns to hunch down away from the stick. If there's still a little too much height on the pony, Roger'll have its feet cut back as far as he dares. Watch that pony go today if you get a chance and have a look at its feet."

I did see the pony go, and I managed to get a close look at it after one class while the groom was sponging him off. Jan was right. Its hoofs were cut back farther than anything I'd ever seen, a lot more than I'd ever have thought possible.

"So how come the pony's not lame?" I asked Jan later.

"Bute, probably," said Jan, busy looking for a bridle in the tack stall. "Bute—that's short for phenylbutazone. It's a medicine used to reduce pain and inflammation. The vet gave it to Sam for the first few days after he hurt his foot.

"But the trouble is that bute can also be used to hide all kinds of problems. Until recently you couldn't show a horse or pony until he'd been off bute for three days, but they've changed the rules and you can imagine what a break this is for people like Roger Hill. He can go ahead now and cut the feet back on that chestnut, fill him full of bute, and show him as sound.

"They're even allowing it to be used on race horses

at some tracks now, which is a scandal. There are horses racing and jumping today that should be home in their stalls in bandages."

Jan found the bridle and straightened the reins. "It's possible, of course, that Roger's using something a lot stronger than bute. He wouldn't dare do this as often with his show horses, because they're spot-checked occasionally for drugs, but he sure uses a lot of different stuff on his ponies. You seldom see the ponies at shows being tested."

"If you know all this, how come he gets away with it?" I was horrified. Jan's face flushed with anger as she answered my question.

"Roger, as they say, has a lot of clout. Meaning he has a lot of very fancy clients with some very fancy connections. Those of us who know what he does haven't got the influence to stop it." Jan went to put the bridle on Whispering Sands. "Get on this pony and warm her up for me, will you, please? She's got a class in twenty minutes and her owner hasn't come yet."

I rode Whispering Sands to a quiet corner of the field and started her into a trot. I looked at some of the other ponies warming up for the next class. I felt uncomfortable and slightly bewildered by what I'd just heard, and I couldn't help looking at the shining ponies in a different way. How many of them were really what they were supposed to be? How many of them should have been lame, but weren't? How many of them were ponies at all?

I broke Whispering Sands into a slow canter. She started to buck and play a little. I had my hands full for the next few minutes, and had to concentrate on what I was doing. Let Roger Hill do things his way; our ponies were fit and sound and properly schooled. The conversation with Jan faded from my mind as the busy day went on.

I still had to get Crumb ready; one of Jan's client ponies had banged himself on the fetlock and couldn't be ridden for a few days, so there'd been an extra stall in the van. Jan suggested I bring Crumb along for a few of the pony classes. He wasn't exactly the prettiest mover in the world, but he could jump like a fiend, and later that morning we had two ties in a jumping class. And Crumb came through with a final clear round to win the blue ribbon and a trophy.

We beat some fantastically good ponies that day, including another of Jan's clients, but everyone seemed genuinely pleased and the other riders walked their own ponies while I tended to Crumb.

He was hot and tired, though I had been as careful with him as I knew how. He'd won jumping classes for me at smaller shows, of course, but the fences had been lower and far less demanding. I sponged him and walked him and wished achingly that he was ten years younger.

When I thought no one was looking, I fed him two carrots from the lovely silver bowl he'd won. I didn't want anyone catching me being so sentimental, but I wanted Crumb to know what his winning meant to me. Jan saw me—she didn't miss much—but she just smiled understandingly and didn't say a word. I hung Crumb's blue ribbon on his stall door and hurried back to help Angie with Sam, who had gone into one of his pony sulks and was refusing to open his mouth for the bit.

## Chapter 7

Horse showing is the same as any other sport. It has its own grapevine, which hums and buzzes with rumors and facts. It took a little while, as these things do, but after I'd been to several shows with the Ashford ponies, I got plugged in and began to hear all kinds of things.

More than anything else, I was curious about Alex,

and I seldom missed a chance to watch Cat Burglar jump. Since one or two of Alex's horses usually traveled with us in Jan's van, they were usually stabled near us at the shows. Alex kept pretty much to himself, and I stayed away from his horses at the stabling area, but there was nothing to stop me from going to the ring when Cat Burglar was entered in a class—and this horse was really something to see.

The day Crumb won his big class and got so tired, I scratched him from the rest of the classes in which he'd been entered so he could rest, and went instead to the main ring to watch Cat Burglar go.

I had already discovered you can't learn much or see as much up in the box seats; many of the parents of Jan's pupils invited us to their boxes, and I went sometimes to be polite, but the people who knew what horse showing was really about generally were down at the rail of the ring and I much preferred to be there myself.

Alex had two jumpers entered that day—a weedy, slightly hysterical black mare named Cantata who jumped like a whirlwind, and Cat Burglar.

Alex rode Cantata first. She knocked down a rail at the in-and-out. Five other horses jumped, and then Alex rode into the ring on Cat Burglar.

You could hear a low hum ripple through the crowd of spectators. But the tall brown horse paid no attention. He stood quietly while Alex took off his black hunt cap and bowed to the judges. The sun glinted on his fair hair. He set his cap firmly back on his head, shortened his reins, and Cat Burglar moved into a canter.

The spectators grew absolutely silent. It was almost as though every person there was holding his breath in anticipation and sheer admiration.

Every now and then a horse like this comes along. Not the flashy, pretty horses or cute little horses that become sentimental favorites of a less knowledgeable crowd. I mean the kind of horse admired by experienced horsemen and horsewomen, owners and riders and grooms and blacksmiths and van drivers—the professional horsemen and the dedicated amateurs, all knowing when Cat Burglar walked into the ring that this was the kind of horse you look for all your life, because if you find one, everything will be different.

I'd been told positively that the horse had come from the west in a cattle car as an unbroken four-year-old. I'd been told he'd been bred in Virginia, raced in Carolina, and imported from Ireland. My favorite story was the one told me by a discouraged groom whose horse had just been beaten throughout an entire show by Cat Burglar. He told me the horse had been sired by the devil out of the night wind—

which makes a fabulous story but sounds a little impractical for a basic breeding program.

The truth seemed to be that this leggy brown horse was just one of a bunch of six or seven others that Alex had bought from a dealer, when he was still just a struggling pro making a buck however he could out of any horse that passed through his hands. As usually happens, some of this bunch weren't worth bothering with. One or two Alex trimmed up and got fat and shiny, and sent off to another part of the country where people talked in thousands instead of hundreds of dollars without turning a hair, and he made some useful money out of those.

Cat Burglar was just one more horse in the bunch. He wasn't much to look at. The only thing that made him different was that when Alex went to fetch him in from the field one night, the horse jumped a few low schooling fences before coming to the pasture gate.

The fences were just jumps stuck up any old way in the field, and they weren't very high. But even I know how seldom a horse without a rider will jump ordinary jumps just for the fun of it—usually they swerve around them without making a thing of it, one way or another.

So when Alex shipped the other horses along to their various destinies, he hung onto this brown horse and started to fool around with him a little. He took him to a few small trial shows and found out exactly what he needed to know. This leggy brown horse that didn't look like any kind of horse at all would jump anything in the world you put him at if you just sat still and let him alone.

Sitting up there in the saddle of this horse and letting him alone was probably the hardest thing Alex ever had to learn to do in his entire life. He was the kind of rider who always had to look busy when he rode—nipping back on the reins, getting a horse up on his toes with his spurs, and forever schooling his horses in dusty back rings at every show.

The grapevine had reported to me (with much chuckling and chortling) that Alex had started out riding Cat Burglar this way, without much success. Then one day he'd taken a crop to the horse for one reason or another. Cat Burglar quietly went on to jump the two schooling fences and continued, just as quietly, on over the ring fence and over a convertible parked beside it. All of this may or may not have been true, but whatever did it, somehow Alex learned to let his horse alone.

As soon as he did, his days on the leaky-roof show circuit were over, and he'd made the big time.

Cat Burglar started to win, and he won from one end of the country to the other. He could be beaten, of course—any living thing can have an off day—but this seldom happened. The prize money piled up and Alex's name and reputation grew along with that of his great horse.

## Chapter 8

Cat Burglar never touched a toe to a jump. He moved over the course like a whisper. Alex pulled up to a trot, rode out of the ring, vaulted off, and handed the horse's reins to Dan. He smiled at the respectful spectators who had drawn back to let him through. Alex had too much sense to swagger, though the set of his back and shoulders was rigid as he walked away with the effort of trying to keep a modest profile.

Dan threw the wide wool cooler over the horse and paused to loosen the girth of the saddle. Cat Burglar turned his lean brown head and looked out over the crowd. There were a few flecks of white foam on the rings of his silvery bit and his nostrils flared slightly. Aside from this, and the slightest quivering of his pricked ears, there was no sign of the effort he'd just put into his jumping.

Dan, the head groom, knew me, of course. He'd seen me almost every day at the stables with Jan and the ponies, and he knew I came to the shows with them, but his eyes slid over me indifferently as he turned and led the horse away. I let out a sigh so deep that it sounded like a groan.

I heard Jan laugh behind me. "What was that for?" she asked.

"Just jealous," I said, embarrassed. "I hope I can get to ride a horse like that one day."

Jan watched Cat Burglar being led back toward the stabling tents. Her expression was thoughtful.

"They don't come like him very often," she said. "You're not alone in wanting that kind. I don't know if it's true or not, but I just heard Alex has been offered half a million dollars for that horse."

"Oh, come on," I said, staring at her. "That's five hundred thousand dollars!" I rolled this over my tongue, trying to decide whether it sounded like more than half a million, or whether it was the other way around.

Not that it mattered, one way or another. The fact was it was so much money that it didn't make any difference. It was all just words and numbers without any real significance as far as my own bewildered mind could tell.

"Alex would have told you," I said finally. "I mean,

that's quite a story. But who'd pay that much for a horse? Other than a race horse, maybe."

"You'd be surprised." Jan and I started walking back to the stables. "Show jumping is getting to be a big sport, and there's a lot of money involved."

"Half a million." I shook my head slowly. "That ought to set Alex up for a few years."

Jan stopped and turned toward me. "But he's refused it," she said.

"Alex? Turned down half a million dollars? For a horse?" I couldn't believe it.

Jan lengthened her stride as we started walking again. She was a lot taller than I was, but with a hop and a skip now and then I managed to keep up with her across the clipped grass of the polo field.

"Maybe he's afraid he'll never find another like Cat," Jan said over her shoulder. "And maybe the whole story isn't true to begin with."

I just shrugged my shoulders and saved my breath. I knew I'd find out sooner or later.


Pelting around after the show ponies in the hot sun that afternoon, I had no time to wonder about Cat Burglar. The heat lay in a suffocating blanket over the flat polo field. The ponies quickly grew sticky with sweat and their riders were cross and the flies were awful. Jan and I sponged the ponies, half-drowned their small riders with fruit juices and iced tea, and tried to keep peace and harmony going in all directions.

Some of the ponies went into a fit of the sulks; so did some of the riders. Unfortunately, the way things always seem to work out, it was usually the sulky rider that had the cheerful pony, and vice versa, except for Sam and his rider, who went their way unperturbed and won several nice ribbons.

These two made the whole afternoon worthwhile, heat and all. At last, toward the end of the day, pale streaks of gray misted the horizon over the trees at the edge of the field, and a sloppy wet breeze started puffing fitfully at the edges of the stabling tents as we began to put the ponies away.

It was terribly hot under the tent. Fortunately the stalls assigned to us were on the outside aisle and the least breeze helped cool our stalls.

A groom carrying a hay net stopped near us and squinted hopefully at the sky. "This ground's like concrete," he said. "We could sure use some rain to soften things up a bit."

"The weather report said showers tonight," Jan said. "Maybe they'll break this awful heat, too."

The groom nodded and departed, looking pleased. Jan smiled. "He takes care of that pretty little chestnut hunter of the Davinos'. The mare's had a terrific case of the quits today—she's stopped or run out in every class. This hard ground is making her feet hurt and she doesn't want to jump. No wonder he's hoping for a little soft mud!"

I went to check Crumb's water bucket to make sure it was full, straightened his sheet, and fluffed up his straw bed a little. I knew he was still tired and would lie down as soon as the evening stables grew quiet. I tended to the other ponies in the stalls beside him, put their halters away in the extra stall we used as a tack room, and then glanced at Cat Burglar, who was in the last stall on the aisle. This made his the corner stall, which was the coolest and most comfortable. Cat Burglar was quietly eating his hay, looking serene and unruffled as always.

The partitions between the stalls were high, but there were gaps between the rough boards of the temporary show stabling. I slipped my hand through and Cat reached out and blew softly on my fingers. "Good night, good horse," I said to him in a low voice. He looked at me for a long moment with his wise, dark eyes, then turned and went back to his hay. I ran to join Jan, who was waiting nearby in her station wagon.

# Chapter 9

**W**e were a long way from home. Too far to drive back and forth each day of this three-day show. But there was a nice motel near the show grounds where most of the show people stayed every year. My room was big, with the air conditioner going full blast when I came in. I dumped my suitcase onto the floor and made a dive for the shower. I stood under the delicious cool water, letting it pour over my hair and all over me for a long time. Dreamily I slopped shampoo into a mountain of squashy suds in my hair and rejumped every wonderful fence in the class I'd won on The Crumb that day.

The glowing silver bowl was the first thing I got out of my suitcase and I put it on the dressing table as I dried my hair. Wonderful Crumb.

Jan pounded on the door a little while later and shouted that she was starving. I hurried guiltily into some clean clothes and we went to have dinner.

The restaurant was jammed with horse-show people and we had a marvelous time, all talking horses, of course. Several people congratulated me on my win with The Crumb, and two separate people even asked me if he were for sale! One was a dealer who handled only good ponies and one was the father of a rider who'd had a bad day on a worse pony. Naturally I said he wasn't for sale, but it was a glorious feeling to be asked, and I floated back to my room later absolutely on top of the world.

Tim came blasting up to the show grounds on his hideous motorcycle the next morning while Jan and I were finishing braiding the last of the ponies' manes. A lot of people left their ponies braided for the duration of the show, but Jan insisted the manes and tails be taken down every night and braided freshly the next morning. It was a pain sometimes, believe me, because it meant extra hours of work each day, but I must admit the ponies always looked nice.

Tim watched in silence as I tied the strong thread around Sam's last braid and patted the braid flat. "Do the kids who ride these creatures have any idea how much work goes into this kind of stuff?" Tim asked as I put the pony back into his stall.

I stopped to think. "I don't really know," I said finally. I went to get The Crumb, handed Tim the lead rope to hold, and started to do up the pony's black mane. "It doesn't really make all that much difference. Even if they don't like doing it, I do, and I get paid for it, too."

Tim sat on a hay bale and fidgeted and asked a

stream of questions until Dan led Cat Burglar from his stall and started to groom him.

"Is that one anything special?" asked Tim. "I can't tell any of them apart."

Keeping my voice down almost to a whisper so Dan wouldn't hear, I told Tim all about Cat Burglar, including the rumor that Alex had been offered half a million dollars for the horse. "That's dumb," said Tim, scowling at Cat from under his shaggy hair. "Who'd want to pay that much money for a horse?"

I didn't confess I'd asked the very same question just the day before. I'd heard a lot since then, mostly at dinner the night before, and I told Tim what I knew as I went on with my work on The Crumb.

There were at least two people after Cat Burglar. One man owned a big show stable full of second-rate horses—horses all of us ungraciously called "charity horses" because they came to the shows and paid their hundreds of dollars of entry fees almost like donations, because they never won any of them back.

The man who owned the stable was getting a little tired of this. He could afford the expense, but it was embarrassing to invite all his business friends to come to sit in his box at the horse shows just to watch his horses get beaten. "So he's gotten a little frantic," I explained, "and he's looking for a horse that can do some winning for him for a change."

I patted The Crumb and started to braid his fore-lock. He put his head down obligingly so I could reach it without having to stand on a bucket as I had to do with some of the other big ponies. "The other offer I know of is from one of the European show jumping teams." The words came out kind of strangely because I had two strands of thread clenched between my teeth, but Tim managed to understand. "I don't know which country it is, but they've got their eye on the next Olympics and they think Cat Burglar might help them out."

"Is he really that good?" asked Tim.

"If you can stand to wait that long, he's jumping in a class at two o'clock and you can see him go." Tim looked stricken; he could seldom stay in one place for more than a short time, especially on weekends, which he usually spent with his motorcycle pals. I'd certainly been surprised to see him at the show that morning. It flashed through my mind that he felt he ought to keep an eye on me, after the incident with the syringe in my pocket earlier that spring. Tim was a dedicated worrier, too, once he'd made up his stubborn mind that there was something he ought to worry about, and he was hard to discourage.

Tim mumbled that he would see how things went,

I finished The Crumb, and we plunged into the morning classes.

The heat was worse than ever. The showers that had been promised through the night had not fallen, the ground was hot and hard, and the ponies and their riders drooped and wilted through their classes. The Crumb and I won a nice second over the outside course and a fourth in a class in the ring, but it was almost too hot for it to matter.

Finally, just before the last class went into the ring before the lunch break, clouds boiled up over the limp trees and dumped buckets of rain for about twenty minutes. As suddenly as they'd come, the clouds disappeared, the sun came out again, and I can hardly begin to tell you what a mess everything was then.

The polo field on which the show was being held hadn't had a drop of rain for weeks. The surface was like concrete under the short grass and it was too hardened to absorb all that rain at once. Sheets of water lay everywhere and very gradually turned the top surface of the ground into a thin layer of greasy mud.

Everything steamed in the humid air. The flags around the main ring hung in sodden folds and even the band sounded murky as it started to play at two o'clock.

There had been a frenzy of activity in the blacksmith shop behind the permanent club stabling all through the lunch break, as shoes were reset on many of the jumpers. Mud calks and sharp heels were added to the shoes to help the horses stay on their feet in the slippery going.

The riders walked the course in the ring, measuring the distance between the jumps and the angle of the turns with extra care.

The band stopped playing, the coaching horn sounded to call the class, and the first horse walked briskly into the ring.

Some of the jumpers had a lot of trouble in the sticky footing. One lost his nerve at the last split second before taking off at a jump, tried to stop, and skidded right through the fence. He scattered rails all over the ring. Another slipped and fell on a turn, but Cat Burglar had little trouble. He was as light and as quick on his feet as his namesake. Alex sat as still as a thief himself and let the horse alone coming into his fences so he could set himself as he liked. Aside from one little bit of a skid turning into the triple in-and-out, which made the horse stumble for one short stride, everything went like cream and Alex rode out of the ring with another clear round behind him.

I was in my favorite spot beside the ring gate, as always. And, as always, Alex vaulted out of the saddle and flipped the reins to Dan, who was waiting with the cooler over his arm. Even though the weather was hot, the coolers went on these good horses as soon as they came out of the ring, to keep their muscles from cramping up. Dan loosened the girth and flung the cooler over Cat Burglar, but instead of leading him away immediately, he stopped to watch the next horse go into the ring.

This was a horse worth watching. Standing still, he looked like the worst kind of clod. His feet were too big, his head was enormous, and his tail hung on behind him like an afterthought. No amount of vitamins or grooming could put a shine on his pale chestnut coat. He looked lonely without a plow.

But he could jump the side of a barn. He had a heart as big as he was and proved beyond doubt that good horses come in all shapes and sizes. He was owned and ridden by a girl who couldn't have weighed more than a hundred pounds, including her boots, which meant she had to carry slabs of lead in her saddle pads to make up the minimum weight of 165 pounds called for in many of the jumping classes. Her big horse pulled like a truck no matter what kind of bit they put on him, and how his rider held him and turned him nobody knew, but he really could jump. And that was all that mattered.

Dan waited to watch the big horse roll into a gallop toward the first jump, with clods of mud spattering away from his big hoofs, and I reached out sneakily to pat Cat Burglar on the shoulder because no one else ever seemed to bother. And as I did I glanced down and saw the puddle of blood in the mud under the horse's front leg.

Cat was standing quite still, watching the horse in the ring, with his intelligent ears pricked in calm attention. He was standing with his weight evenly on both front legs, so the cut couldn't have been bothering him. But it was very deep—a half-moon gash on the heel of his left foreleg.

My first reaction was to kneel down for a closer look. I started to, then changed my mind, knowing how Alex and Dan both felt about anyone coming near the precious charge. "Hey, Dan," I said instead. "This horse is hurt."

Dan spun around, took one look at the injured leg, and hustled the patient horse away. I watched them go and was enormously relieved to see that the horse wasn't limping. Even Alex couldn't have gone on jumping a lame horse, no matter how important the class.

From the wild burst of applause in the grandstand I knew the big chestnut horse had made a clean round and so there would be at least one jump-off to break the tie in this class.

The horse squelched out of the ring through the heavy mud at the gate and the pool of blood from Cat Burglar's leg was covered over.

In spite of the sloppy footing, five horses had clear rounds over the tremendous course. The jumps were raised higher and spread still wider. The horses collected near the ring gate and went in one at a time to jump again.

This time they were jumping against time. If there were two or more clear rounds, the fastest time would determine the winner. Cat Burglar trotted into the ring wearing bell boots, which buckled loosely above his front hoofs to protect his heels. I could see the flash of a white bandage under the left boot just before it got soaked in mud as the horse moved into a canter in the ring.

Though the cut had looked deep and unpleasant—Cat Burglar must have grabbed the heel of his front foot with a hind toe when he slipped during his first round—it certainly didn't bother the horse; he moved and jumped with his usual grace. He never seemed to hurry. Alex cut corners and took one horrendously big stone wall almost at right angles, which would have been enough to bring almost any ordinary horse down, even in perfect footing—but Cat always seemed to have a foot just at the right place to keep his balance as he landed, and he flew past the electronic timer and left the ring a full three seconds faster than his nearest rival.

The huge chestnut fell over the brush and rails and for a few seconds his rider was buried under flying hoofs and splintered rails. But she reappeared grinning, covered every inch with mud, and patted her bewildered horse sympathetically as she led him from the ring. It has always amazed me how surprised a horse looks after he's had a fall, almost as though he's trying to remember what happened so he won't make the same mistake again. Maybe that's what makes the good jumpers as good as they are.

The three other tied horses had clear rounds, but slower times, and Cat Burglar went back into the ring for another blue ribbon. He cantered around the ring to wild applause with the blue ribbon fluttering from his bridle and with Alex clutching a huge silver cup and his hat in his hand, while a gray and a bay and a chestnut cantered humbly behind him.

# Chapter 10

Tim had left the show grounds earlier that morning, but, much to my surprise, he had come back to see Cat Burglar jump, and when he came up to me after the class, he was grinning with excitement.

"That horse would have made one heck of a basketball player," he said. Next to motorcycles, basketball is Tim's undying passion. He couldn't have given the horse a greater compliment.

"Just wait till tomorrow," I said to him as we walked back to the stabling tents. "Tomorrow's the big one, the International Gold Cup. There are two horses here that were flown down from Canada just for this one class, and one from Mexico, and I don't know where else. It's even going to be on television."

"Do you think I could meet this Alex person?" said Tim. "You're moving in exalted circles, my girl."

He glanced at me and tried to sound unconcerned. "No more needles in empty barns, Cindy? Every sport has its strange ones, don't forget. Big prize money can mean big troubles. It's happened before."

"Not in horse shows," I said crossly. I swung around to face him. "In the first place, I don't have anything at all to do with Alex or Cat Burglar. They won't let me even go near the horse, if that makes you feel any better. I work with Jan and the ponies and the children, I've made some wonderful new friends and I have a lot of fun with my Crumb, and that's all I do."

"Yeah," said Tim, jamming his hands into his pockets. I gritted my teeth and regretted, for the thousandth time, having been so stupid as to empty my pockets in front of Tim as I'd done. I had hoped he'd forget, and I'd never told him about seeing the van in the back field that night.

I was furious. Furious because Alex and Dan still made me uneasy, though I would barely admit this, even to myself. Furious because Tim kept bringing all of it back. "You don't have to come here if you don't like it," I said stiffly. "I like horses and you like motorcycles. Why don't you just get on yours and go away and let me alone?"

I left Tim standing at the edge of the soggy polo field and went to The Crumb for comfort. He was half-dozing in the corner of his stall, but he nickered softly as I came in and put his muzzle up to my cheek and blew softly down the back of my collar. I fussed over him and picked out his feet and brushed him down and soon felt much better.

The Horse Show Committee cancelled the pony classes and all the Junior classes for the rest of the show because the mud was so slippery. The announcement had been made over the loudspeaker just before the jumping class started. As Tim would have put it, there was no use wrecking the kids for a few lousy blue ribbons; the mud made the courses unsafe, especially for the inexperienced junior riders. I was just starting to take The Crumb's braided mane down when Jan came flying into the stall with her eyes bright with excitement.

"Don't do that!" she said breathlessly. "You'll never believe what's happened! They've just finished adding up the points for the pony classes and your pony's tied for Champion!"

"But we only went in three classes, and we didn't do all that well—" I stared at Jan, stunned. I'd done my share of winning at small shows, of course, but this kind of show was way out of my league. The only reason I was here at all was because of the extra stall in the van, and Jan and I had agreed it was a shame to let it go to waste.

But it was true. That one terrific jumping class we'd won and the two other ribbons we'd picked up had given Crumb enough points to tie him with a fantastic gray pony from Maryland, who was the high-score award leader so far for the year in the large pony division.

Jan tacked up my pony for me as I tried to scrub some of the mud off my boots, straighten my hair, and generally make myself look more presentable. The Crumb looked mildly surprised at my nervousness, but he gathered himself together and trotted smartly to the ring where the judges were waiting to break the tie.

The gray pony was beautiful, as one would expect. But he didn't like the mud. Crumb, who was used to going everywhere with me in all kinds of weather, slopped willingly through the puddles while the gray pony skipped and jumped around them. Crumb walked, trotted, and cantered without a mistake, and it was only a few minutes before the blue, red, and yellow streamers of the Championship ribbon were hanging from his bridle. The girl on the gray smiled her congratulations, the band played and the soggy flags tried to wave, and it was all sheer heaven. There was no question about it. Winning was heady stuff.

A photographer from a newspaper asked my name, took a photograph of me and The Crumb wearing his Championship ribbon, and promised the picture would be in the paper on Monday.

Tim was ecstatic. Though I would never have told him so, I was glad he'd stayed to share our triumph. He helped me sponge the pony off and we walked him, and then Tim and I stood in companionable silence as I let the pony graze a little to finish cooling him out. We watched the rain clouds build up again and when it started to sprinkle, I led Crumb back into his stall.

Tim waited while I took the pony's halter off, hugged him, and latched the stall door. We started toward the hamburger stand. I had one and Tim had two, and we went together to watch the class going on in the ring.

The light sprinkle turned to heavy rain and then fell in sheets. The young hunters in the ring were not happy with conditions either underfoot or overhead. They squealed and shied and shook their heads—I wonder why horses so hate to get their ears wet?—and most of the riders and the judges, too, were smiling (except for the one or two riders who looked as though they were about to be bucked off, which made them understandably a little nervous). Most people seem to think that rodeo horses are the hardest buckers of all, but a young, fit, well-fed, highly bred Thoroughbred can make a rodeo horse look like an amateur if he puts his mind to it.

The judges quickly picked their winners before any of the riders came unglued. The horses tiptoed or floundered out of the ring, depending on their natures, and then the storm was over and the sun came out again.

"I'm going on home," said Tim, squinting at the

sky. "It'll take me over an hour, even if the sun stays out. Any messages for Mom and Dad?"

"Tell them about Crumb," I said. "I know they'll be pleased. Tell them I'm fine and that I'll be home for dinner tomorrow. All the excitement's over." Tim went off with a wave of his hand to get his motorcycle and I turned back to watch the next class in the ring.

# Chapter 11

We went back to the motel that evening, and I was lying dreamily on top of the bed, still winning the jumping class over and over again on Crumb, when I heard a pounding on my door.

"Hey, are you asleep?" Jan shouted.

As I opened the door to let her in the sky flickered with a flash of distant lightning. Jan hurried into the room.

"I just wanted to let you know that I'm going back to the show grounds for a minute," Jan said. "I left my other suitcase in the tack stall and I need some of the things in it."

"Wait a second," I said. "I'll get my jacket and go with you." Jan protested, but not with much conviction. It was dark and kind of spooky, and I knew she really wanted company.

There were rumbles of thunder and a lot more lightning as we drove the short distance to the show grounds. "Maybe these storms will clear the air," Jan said, turning through the gates. "Too late now for the ground to dry, but maybe it won't be so hot tomorrow."

When we got to the field where the stabling tents stood and got out of the car, the lightning was sharp and fierce. A few dim bulbs burned high in the tent, but most of the stalls were in shadow. We left the car lights on but moved quietly so as not to disturb the horses. Some were lying down; others put their heads over their stall doors to inspect us as we passed.

Jan took a small flashlight out of her pocket. She checked our ponies as we went down the line. They were all lying down, but Crumb knew my voice, even in a whisper, and got to his feet. He stretched and came over to the door. I gave him a lump of sugar and rubbed him behind the ears as I waited for Jan to get her suitcase from the tack stall.

When she came back I could see, even in the dim light, that she was concerned. "Cat Burglar's in an awful state," she said. "He's afraid of the lightning."

I gave Crumb one last pat and followed Jan to the corner stall and looked inside.

Poor Cat was huddled in the far corner of the stall with his legs all bunched beneath him. He was quivering with fright and his neck was shining with sweat. There was another blazing flash of lightning; the horse crouched and threw his head up. His eyes were rolling—you could see the whites all around them.

"Poor thing," Jan said. Murmuring quiet, comforting sounds, she slipped into the stall and patted the trembling horse. " 'Sakes,' " she said to him, " 'it's only weather.' " But Cat Burglar was not about to be comforted, even by Robert Frost. Jan quoted the whole poem to the horse, but just as she reached the last line the lightning came again and the horse went on shaking.

"This won't do," Jan said at last. "He'll be a wreck by morning. He's going to be worn out, and he's got the Gold Cup class tomorrow." She frowned thoughtfully at the horse and then nodded her head.

"Cindy, if it's all right with you, I've got an idea. Crumb doesn't mind lightning, does he?"

"Not at all," I told her. "He's been out with the cows a lot at night during the summer and weather never bothers him."

"Would you mind, then, if we switched stalls? We could put your pony in here and move Cat Burglar into your pony's stall, away from this corner, where the lightning won't be so bright."

"Sure thing." I knew it wouldn't make any difference to Crumb, one way or another, so with the aid of Jan's gradually expiring flashlight and the streaks of lightning, we found the proper halters and exchanged stalls. I tossed an extra armload of hay in for Crumb, who started munching peacefully, as I knew he would. Even Cat Burglar, once he was away from the outside corner stall, began to unwind a little and managed a wisp or two of hay.

We waited for a while, sitting on a bale of hay in the tack stall, listening to the gentle sounds of horses in the night. The lightning flickered outside the tent, and an occasional breeze rustled the trees. Jan's flashlight died of exhaustion; Crumb turned around in his new stall once or twice and then lay down with a sigh of contentment.

We heard Cat move around uneasily at first, but he soon settled down, drank a few gulps of water, and then we heard the sound of steady, tranquil munching of hay coming softly from his stall.

"That's better," Jan said. "I'm glad we changed them. I'll explain it to Alex in the morning." She stood up stiffly. "Come on, we'd better get some sleep." We went quietly back to the car, where the lights we'd forgotten were still burning bravely but a little paler than before. Fortunately the battery wasn't dead, and we finally got back to the motel and went, at last, to bed.

Jan and I were still half-asleep the next morning when we turned in through the gates and half-bumped, half-slid the station wagon through the mud on the way to the tents.

My wandering wits were certainly not in focus—we hadn't even had breakfast—so Jan and I both just sat for some moments after she'd parked the car, staring at the knots of people beside the first tent. There was always activity on any horse-show grounds just after dawn, of course. The grooms were always up early, feeding and watering and starting the thousand and one things that had to be done before the show's morning session began. But this early work was quietly done. There wasn't any real hustle or bustle due for at least another two hours. But as we sat in the car and watched blankly, we saw a man running, and we heard shouting, and there were two people waving their arms excitedly. Several horses were neighing with a high-pitched, nervous sound. Horses always seem to know when there is something wrong.

The clot of people moved away from where they had been standing. And I noticed two things at exactly the same time. The running man was carrying a black bag in his hand—and the door to the stall was open, just swinging open, gaping open on its hinges, and it was Crumb's corner stall.

Jan and I shot out of the car and raced across to the stables. Neither of us said a word. We reached the bunch of people near the stall and I barged my way through. I felt someone grab at my shoulder and I heard someone shout, "Keep that kid out of there!" but I dug my elbows into various ribs and plunged through to the open stall door.

Crumb was dead. I knew he was dead the instant I saw him. The pony was stretched out on his side and the doctor was kneeling beside him, shaking his head.

"Old pony. Just died in his sleep, I guess," I heard someone say. But the vet went on shaking his head and he looked up as Jan came to stand beside me in horrified, frozen silence.

"He's mine," I said, and I went into the stall. I heard my voice as though it were coming from somewhere else; it didn't sound like me. I heard the whispery rustle of the straw under my boots, and that seemed real, but as I knelt beside Crumb and put my hand on his dear neck and found it cool and strange to touch, that didn't seem real. I didn't feel sad. I didn't feel like crying. For a few long minutes, I simply didn't feel anything at all.

# Chapter 12

I touched Crumb's shoulder with my fingertips. "I killed him, I guess," I said to the doctor in a very matter-of-fact voice. At least it started out that way, but sort of wobbled toward the end. I cleared my throat. "He wasn't a young pony any more. I'm sure I asked him to do too much for me. I shouldn't have brought him here, I shouldn't have shown him yesterday—" I couldn't go on. I felt as though I were choking.

There were murmurs of sympathy and agreement from the people crowding behind me at the stall door.

"You didn't kill him," the doctor said, shutting his bag with a snap and getting to his feet. His voice was sharp and angry.

"Cindy, look over here." Jan's voice sounded angry, too, and I couldn't understand. I turned around slowly, feeling so miserably guilty that it took a few moments to really hear what Jan was saying.

"Cindy," Jan said again impatiently. "Look over here! Don't touch it. Just look."

To be honest, I thought she'd gone stark, raving mad. In the dim light of early morning, the corners of the stall were still in shadow. I couldn't understand why the lights weren't on, but nothing else was making any sense either. I got up and went over to where Jan was standing near the feed tub in the corner. She gestured with her hand and I finally saw what she and the vet had seen—the drooping line of a sagging electric wire, just over the tub. At its lowest part the covering of the wire was frayed and torn, and there was a glint of bare wire in two or three places.

"He chewed it," I whispered. My lips felt numb.

"Of course he did," Jan said crisply. "The chances are that any pony would. And once he got through the covering and down to the bare wire, it killed him."

"The ground is damp," said the doctor, "and your pony was wearing metal shoes, of course. At least I can promise you he didn't suffer. Once he bit down to the bare wire, he was dead. Instantly."

Jan and the doctor left together to make a report after cautioning me to leave everything alone. I didn't want to go with them. I stood staring at the dangling, deadly wire for a long time, then I left the stall and carefully shut the door. Even though my common sense told me that Crumb was not going to get up and come trotting out after me, it seemed funny to go away and leave him in the stall with the door open.

I walked out onto the polo field where the sun was

just beginning to shine on the white-fenced ring. Though the ground was still muddy, the red and white flags marking the outside course and the horse-show banners by the ring were beginning to dry out and lift lightly in the early breeze. The last traces of blue mist were lifting from the edges of the field. It was going to be a beautiful day.

A wonderful day for a horse show.

I sat down on a chair near the judges' stand, put my face in my hands, and cried.

Electricians' trucks came tearing up the club drive with their emergency lights flashing. I wondered bitterly what all the hurry was about. Crumb was dead and none of their hurrying was going to bring him back. Ladders shot up in several places. I recognized the show manager's Jeep and then two long, shining cars came sliding up to the tent. Show officials, I guessed. And then a police car. In spite of having cried so hard I felt soggy all over, I had to giggle just once. Jan must be on a rampage.

I saw her come to the edge of the polo field and wave to me. I waved in answer and started back. "It's all very complicated," Jan said as I got nearer. "Are you okay now?" I nodded.

"Good," she said. "This is all a terrible mess, of course. The show manager is insisting the wire must have blown down last night during one of the thunderstorms. The electricians are saying this is impossible; that they've wired these same tents for every show in the area, for years, including one in a near-hurricane, and that they know their job and how dangerous sagging wires are near horses. So the whole thing is impossible."

"Then I suppose they mean Crumb isn't really dead, because the wire couldn't have come down."

"Exactly."

We got near the stall where there was an absolute jumble of people. "They want your permission before they move him," Jan said, as briskly as possible.

I stopped and stared at her. "I hadn't thought of that yet," I said. "What will they do with him?" I started feeling teary all over again. "I always thought he'd be buried on Mr. Martin's farm when he died."

Jan shook her head sadly. "It's too far away."

My knees felt funny. I'd known Crumb wasn't young, I'm not a complete dope about death, and I knew someday the pony would have to be put down —but someday was always far in the future, a sort of walking into the sunset kind of thing, with the mists rising and Crumb sleeping forever under his favorite tree in the cow pasture.

"No dog food. No soap," I said with a croak. "Not for Crumb."

"I'll see what they're planning to do," said Jan. "Wait here."

I sat down on the field, not caring that I'd get grass stains and mud on my riding breeches. I struggled to be sensible and see the practical aspects of the problem. Even though Crumb was only a pony, he was a very big pony, and he couldn't just be picked up and carried home in the back of a station wagon.

Jan came hurrying back. "The president of the club just arrived," she reported breathlessly. "And he's mad enough to spit nails. He wants to tell you himself how sorry he is this happened, he knows how awful this must be for you, and he wants to know if you would let the club have Crumb buried right here on the place, next to his own favorite old hunters and polo ponies—"

She stopped, and there were tears in her eyes, too. I nodded and Jan left, and I wept again briefly and went to say good-bye to Crumb. Someone had spread a cooler over him and the red and white plaid looked slightly ridiculous on the dead pony. I shrugged my shoulders and turned away. Crumb wasn't even there any more. No matter where they put him, I knew he would always be back under his own huge maple tree in my mind.

I said the right things. I thanked the club president, who looked so upset that I felt sorry for *him*. He talked about insurance, and a passing groom stopped to make the mistake of saying that Crumb was only a kid's old pony and couldn't have been of much value. Jan exploded in a tearing rage and the club president hurriedly suggested we all go have a cup of coffee and he swept Jan and me off in his car, which was a great relief to me, because I did not want to see them taking Crumb—or what was left of him— away.

## Chapter 13

I called my parents from the clubhouse to tell them what had happened. No, I didn't want to come right home, I told them. Both Mom and Dad offered to come get me. But I said I'd rather stay at the show and keep busy and come home with Jan that night. Jan spoke to them after I was done, explained again what had happened, and eventually got them calmed down to a reasonable degree.

I had a cup of tea, but I couldn't manage to swallow anything else. Jan and the club president had breakfast. Gradually the talk turned from Crumb's awful accident to the big Gold Cup class to be held that afternoon.

"Show jumping is an extremely popular spectator sport in Europe," the club president said enthusiastically. "We're trying to build it up over here, and it's classes like our Gold Cup that will get people interested. All the big newspapers are sending sportswriters to cover it, and I suppose you know it's going to be on television." He reached over and patted my hand absently. "Naturally it's a terrible thing that your pony was in Cat Burglar's stall when that wire came down last night, but what a loss it would have been for Alex Russell, and for all show jumping, if Cat Burglar had been killed instead!"

I put my hands in my lap and scrunched down in my chair.

The club president leaned forward and lowered his voice. He was obviously very impressed by what he was going to tell us. "I know Alex has been under a lot of pressure to sell that horse, and he's turned down every offer that's been made. But I heard last night at the Horse Show Ball that the captain of a South American jumping team is flying up to talk to Alex after the show. And that Alex just might be persuaded to let the horse go."

"Let the horse go," Jan repeated softly. She smiled at me and winked. Rumors were flying, as they had been for months. And anybody offered half a million dollars for a horse was hardly "letting it go."

When we got back to the stabling tents, everything seemed practically normal. Cat Burglar was still in Crumb's old stall between Sam and Whispering Sands. I peeked into the corner stall. It was empty. The drooping wire was gone and the electricity was back on again all through the stables.

In spite of my wanting to keep busy, there was nothing for me to do. The ponies didn't need me. They were lazily finishing the last of their breakfast hay. Dan brought Cat Burglar out of the stall and started to groom him, hissing softly under his breath at each stroke of the brush. The big horse tossed his head to flip his lead rope into the air and then he caught it between his teeth and shook it gently, like a puppy playing with a toy. A lot of horses and ponies like to play with their lead ropes now and then, but Cat Burglar never let his alone. I'd heard Dan cussing to himself a number of times as he searched for a new lead rope for Cat in the tack room, and once a new stable boy had left Cat's bridle hanging just outside his stall door, where the horse could reach it, and it was in tatters on the floor of his stall when it was finally found.

The morning classes had started in the ring. I

wandered over to watch them. Everyone at the show seemed to have heard about Crumb. There wasn't an exhibitor at the ring who didn't say something kind to me about him.

The television crew were setting up their cameras at the side of the ring, getting ready for the Gold Cup in the afternoon. There seemed to be snaking black wires crawling everywhere, which gave me the creeps, so I wandered out to the far edge of the polo field to watch some of the show jumpers being exercised. I recognized many of them. Photographs of many of these same riders and their horses, cut out from every magazine I could get my hands on, covered one entire wall of my room.

The trickle of cars turning into the show grounds turned into a stream, and then into a flood. Special police waved their arms and blew their whistles, trying to keep things orderly, but some of the drivers moved out of line and ended up axle-deep in mud out by the pony rings, which were closed off because of the soft ground.

Back at the main ring, the lunch break had already started, and the jump crew were setting up the course for the Cup. Tubs of flaming red geraniums marked the turns of the course. Gaily striped rails, wide white gates, a forbidding gray stone wall, and a wishing well full of flowers began to go up in the muddy ring.

Some of the show jumper riders were being interviewed by the television sportscaster in front of one of the cameras. I drifted over to listen. His oily voice asked the usual stupid questions and then he answered most of them himself. The riders, courteous as always, struggled to look interested and polite.

Finally the sportscaster asked one last question, ran out of breath, and waved the microphone toward the patient riders.

"The horses to watch especially today?" The captain of our international team gave the question his careful attention. He named a number of famous horses and riders. I felt a shiver of excitement go down my back; I'd had no idea so many of them were here at the show. Then the captain paused for a moment, and added, "You can't overlook Cat Burglar, that great horse of Alex Russell's. He hasn't competed in many international classes so far, but I don't know when I've seen a more promising jumper. I have the feeling he's going to give all of us a lot of trouble today. He's going to be hard to beat."

The sportscaster interrupted. "I heard that horse was sold last night for half a million dollars. That's an awful lot of money for a horse, isn't it?"

"I should say that depends on how badly you want him," the captain answered with a reserved smile. The sportscaster laughed loudly. "And there you have it, ladies and gentlemen. The opinions of some of the finest jumping riders in the world! Good luck to each and every one of you!" The little red light on top of the television camera blinked off and the announcer turned away, dismissing the riders with a brief wave of his hand. They chatted quietly among themselves as they watched the jump crew finishing setting up the course.

"The first in-and-out looks short," said the girl who owned the big chestnut that had fallen the day before.

She was right. The jump crew rolled up the measuring tape, moved one of the jumps, and measured the distance between them again. The course designer checked the measurement, nodded, and went on to the next jump.

A few minutes later the last jump was checked and riders went into the ring to walk the course. They paced off the distance between the jumps, walked back to study the turns, and the girl with the big chestnut stood for several long moments, frowning at the first in-and-out. I felt sorry for her. It came at a tough spot, just off a sharp turn after a wide triple bar, and it was going to take some quick and clever riding to get her big horse together in time for such a trappy fence.

It was a demanding course, but as I rode over it

in my mind, I longed for the day I might know enough, and be good enough, to show a horse in a class like this, myself.

My heart suddenly ached for Crumb and it ached for me, too. I thought of his empty stall at home. I wished fiercely I could have him back, in exchange for any glorious show jumping career. And then I wondered, a little bitterly, how I was going to manage this fantastic career I had in mind without anything to ride.

I gave an enormous sigh. The man standing beside me looked at me a little strangely, and then the band began to play.

## Chapter 14

The horses were ridden into the ring for the opening parade. Spectators were jammed into the stands and around the ring. Everyone applauded; the horses danced and shied a little with the sunlight gleaming on their coats and winking bright flashes from their polished bits. The riders, some of them wearing black coats and some wearing scarlet, smiled and quietly soothed their horses. Cat Burglar shook his lean head and half-reared once or twice; I wondered if the drums of the band reminded him of the thunder and lightning the night before.

The horses left the ring and the music stopped. The show grounds were tense and silent with anticipation; you could even hear the snapping of the small flags beside the jumps. The ringmaster in his scarlet coat lifted the long, golden coaching horn to his lips and the notes of the horn shimmered in the quiet air. A horse whinnied longingly from a far tent—probably a hunter, listening for the sound of foxhounds to answer the horn. In the expectant hush we could hear silvery rings of an anvil from the blacksmith shop, and then the first horse entered the ring for the class.

A ring steward made a last quick check of the electronic timer, the judges signaled they were ready, and the gray horse in the ring started over the course.

This short-backed, handsome gray stallion jumped as though he were rejoicing with every stride he took and with every fence he met and conquered. He folded his knees right up to his chin and sailed over his fences in a faultless round that brought cheers from the crowd.

One by one the other horses followed, each one moving and jumping in a different way, all of them meeting the challenge of the course with a cock of an ear and a wise understanding of the task set for them. Most of the riders were very good; some were even better. All of them rode with fierce concentration, tact, skill, and incredible courage. Some of them were unlucky and their horses rolled a rail off a jump; one or two made mistakes in their timing, got their horses into their jumps on an off stride, and still managed a clear round.

There was hardly a sound as they jumped except for the breathing of the horses and the soft hoofbeats; occasionally a rider would speak to an impatient horse in a low voice on a turn; once there was a light splash as a horse dropped the toe of one hind hoof into the water jump, and sometimes there was the hollow ringing sound of a hit rail dropping to the ground.

There was a tall dark bay from Canada that jumped as though he had wings. The big chestnut ridden by the girl thundered his way around the course like an express train, never touched a toe to a fence, and left the crowd cheering as he trotted triumphantly from the ring.

Cat Burglar jumped the huge course like a feather. Even Alex, who usually kept an expressionless face, had to look pleased as he left the ring. Altogether, eleven horses had no faults and were called to jump again.

The high fences were raised still higher, the wide fences were spread still wider. The breeze dropped and the afternoon grew hotter, but the mud in the ring, cut by the flying hoofs of the jumping horses, grew deeper and even more slippery. The girl on the enormous chestnut kept her horse tidily collected and carefully balanced, and had a second clear round in good time. But another rider missed his timing at a triple in-and-out, managed the first two jumps, but fell at the third. The horse was led from the ring hobbling on three legs with his rider walking beside him, frantic with worry. "It was my fault, it was all my fault, I didn't get him into it right," the rider kept saying. The show veterinarian ran to meet the injured horse near the ring gate where I was standing in my favorite spot.

"It's not serious," I heard him say after a few moments. "He's got a deep overreach—look, his bell boot tore when he fell and he's got a bad cut on his heel. He'll be pretty sore for a bit, but the lameness won't last very long. Let's get him back to his stall and I'll take care of him there. Don't worry. These things hurt a lot at first, but nothing's broken." They loosened the horse's girth and led him slowly away.

Again there was a puddle of blood in the mud by the gate, just as there'd been with Cat Burglar the day before. Again it was covered by fresh hoofprints as the next horse cantered into the ring.

Five horses had had clear rounds for the second time and had to jump again, with the fences raised still higher. This round, though, would be the last, as each horse was timed electronically, and in case of a tied score, the horse with the shortest time would be the winner.

The compact, brilliant gray stallion had a fantastic round that brought people to their feet with excitement as he flashed across the line at the end of the course. It looked as though he'd be impossible to beat. Cat Burglar walked into the ring while the stands were still buzzing over the gray's performance. Alex waited. The spectators grew silent, the judges signaled, and Cat Burglar moved into a quiet canter.

I don't know how he did it. Neither Alex nor the horse seemed to feel any pressure; no matter what other faults Alex may have had, he had nerves of steel. And Cat Burglar jumped with the precision and the timing of a watch. The tall brown horse floated over the enormous jumps as though time were standing still for him. He put in three smooth galloping strides where other horses had needed five. He came off the ground at his jumps after each turn from a distance that left people gasping, and finished the course four-fifths of a second faster than the great little gray.

The crowd exploded into cheers and shouts. The band crashed into music as Cat Burglar trotted smoothly from the ring.

The winners were called back. The cup really was gold; anyway, it certainly looked like gold as it was presented to Alex. The rider on the gray horse shook hands with Alex and then accepted the red second-place ribbon with a grin. With Cat Burglar leading the way, the eight winning horses cantered around the ring single file, with the streamers of their well-earned ribbons dancing on their bridles.

The horses didn't play or shy this time. Even Cat Burglar paid no attention to the drums as he passed the band; all the horses were a little tired. It had been a sensational class.

Dan took Cat Burglar's reins as Alex swung out of the saddle and hurried off to be interviewed on television. Cat Burglar was hot and sweaty all over and I followed him back to the stabling tents. Maybe Dan would, just this once, let me help with the horse.

Dan turned my offer down with a sharp shake of his head, threw the cooler over Cat Burglar, and went to get a bucket of hot water. I glanced at the ponies in my charge; they were bored in their stalls, but perfectly fine. Crumb's empty stall looked so bare and lonely that I went in to fuss over Sam, straightening his sheet and brushing out his mane and tail, which were still wavy from being braided for the show.

The show was nearly over. We'd be loading up the van very soon, taking the ponies and Cat Burglar home. I still had to face Crumb's empty stall at my own house, which would look lonelier than his stall here at the show. There'd be Crumb's bridle and saddle to clean one last time and put away, the stall to sweep out and close up, unused grain and hay and bedding to be given away before it went sour—no Crumb to finish the grain, no friendly whinny to greet me when I got home each day from school.

I hurried out of Sam's stall to find something—anything—to do.

The weary Cat Burglar was standing near the tent while Dan sponged him off with hot water. One of the stable boys was holding him. Dan pressed the sweat scraper gently against the horse's wet shoulder and the water trickled from the scraper, leaving fresh clean paths on the sleek coat.

When he had finished, Dan told the boy to lead the horse quietly in the shade and keep him walking until he was dry and cool. The boy nodded indifferently, gave Cat a yank on his halter, and towed him away.

As much as I disliked Dan, I knew he'd have had a fit if he'd seen the boy's bored, disinterested look.

Whatever Dan was like, he was fierce about the care of the horses in his charge. But someone was having trouble loading a young horse into a van. He shouted to Dan, who went to lend a hand.

I saw the boy sneak a look out of the corner of his eye as Dan hurried away and, as soon as he was out of sight, the boy stopped, leaned against a tree, and lit a cigarette.

The flies were terrible. The rain and heat had brought them out in vicious clouds. I had put fly repellent on the ponies in my care and they were in shady stalls, so the flies were pretty well leaving them alone. But poor Cat Burglar, hot and tired as he was after his terrific effort, stamped and kicked and shook his head as the flies attacked him out in the sun.

It wasn't fair. I was hot and tired, too, and sad and cross, and I couldn't bear it. I started over toward the horse.

As I got near him I stopped again, uncertainly. I wasn't quite sure how I was going to give Alex's stable boy orders he should have been obeying in the first place. I watched for a moment, trying to make up my mind what to do, and I noticed something peculiar about the way the brown horse was acting. The fat, green-headed horseflies have a particularly sharp bite. There were two of them on the lower part of Cat's left front leg and he was paying no attention to them at all. He was stamping and kicking the flies away from his other three legs, but he didn't seem to mind the two I could plainly see.

I took a step backward, turned, and went into Crumb's empty stall. I sat down in the corner and put my head in my hands. Wisps of questions floated through my mind like puffs of smoke. Why couldn't Cat Burglar feel the fly bites on his left front leg? And shouldn't he have limped, at least just a little, when he'd cut his heel so badly on the same leg in the jumping class the day before? It didn't make sense.

I was so tired my bones ached, but I couldn't sit still. I got up restlessly and went to look at Cat again. The boy was moving him now, walking him in the shade as he'd been told to do, and I could see the flash of the fresh white bandage over the cut on the horse's heel.

Jan had told me the horse had been lame on and off last winter, but that he'd suddenly gotten better in the spring. Lucky Alex. The stable fire had killed almost all his horses—Cat Burglar had been saved only because a stranger had gotten him out in time. Lucky Alex, again. And then, last night, Jan had moved the horse from his stall because of the lightning and my pony had died instead.

Creepy. I felt goosebumps prickle my arms and I shivered. All of it was creepy, and I was tired of my gloomy thoughts. I hurried out into the sunlight and went to get a Coke.

I went to hold a friend's pony while she bandaged his legs and tail and then helped her load him into the trailer. "Thanks," she said. "See you next Saturday at the 4-H show! You're not going to a big show instead, are you? You'll be there with Crumb?" She stopped and her eyes filled with tears. "I'm sorry," she said. "For just a minute I forgot. It's going to seem so strange not having him around."

I just nodded. I couldn't trust myself to speak, so I just waved good-bye. Everybody was going to miss Crumb, but tears weren't going to help.

I felt a flicker of anger. Alex certainly didn't seem to be sorry. If he was, he hadn't said so; at least, not to me. Would he have been sorry if Cat had died instead? He'd probably just have been mad because his horse was worth so much money. Half a million dollars' worth of horse, zonked in his stall.

I brooded. I stood in the field, half-watching the vans getting ready to pull out. The ground had been torn and churned into a sea of choppy mud. I heard someone shout and moved out of the way as a huge tractor lurched past me on the way to tow out a stuck van.

I glanced at my watch and started back to the tents. Time to get our own ponies loaded and on their way home. The tack trunks could go in the empty stall in the van instead of in the center aisle, which made Jan nervous. If the van had to stop suddenly it might throw one of the ponies off balance and pitch him forward; if the safety strap across his chest broke, which sometimes happened, he could fall on a trunk and get hurt—

Worry, worry, worry. And what good did it do? I had a bitter taste in my mouth. I kicked a clod of dirt with my muddy boot. An enormous trailer hitch with tinted windows, full of show horses from Ohio, ground its way past me and threw mud in my direction from its huge wheels. In my fury at everything I shouted words at it even Tim didn't know I knew— but nothing made me feel any better.

How come people like Alex had all the luck? I was beginning to shake with rage and frustration. I must have looked like a maniac screaming unheard words in that muddy field, but I didn't care. I'd loved my pony, I'd taken good care of him and treated him kindly and called for the vet whenever anything went wrong, while the Alexes of the world went on their lucky way over the broken-down horses they ruined without a second thought. "Alex is a hard man on a horse." That's what they said. "They never last long in his hands."

Ruined, ruined, crippled, and dead. "Something is wrong with so-and-so's horse, he's lame." Or hurt. Or he isn't trying any more. And how many times had so-and-so's horse had a funny little accident that just happened to be fatal?

That rugged black show jumper I'd seen last spring, when the show season was starting—he'd been tied to a stable tent stake with just a rope around his neck. I'd gone running to find his groom; I was wild with worry. "Don't you know that's not the way to treat a good horse?" I'd shouted at the stable boy who was mucking out the horse's stall. "He's going to get hurt!"

"No kidding," said the boy with a grin. "How about that?" And he went on with his work. I'd stood at the door of the stall and just stared at the boy's back. I couldn't understand what he meant. The black horse had won and won all winter, but he'd gone lame and had been stopping at his fences at the last few shows and I'd heard his owner was looking for another horse. "If I were you, I'd mind my own business," the stable boy said to the manure basket, loud enough for me to hear, and an hour later the black horse was dead. He'd "accidentally" broken his neck. The insurance company paid and a few weeks later his rider appeared on an expensive new horse and began winning again.

"You make your own luck." Some of these so-called horsemen made themselves a funny kind of luck. I went to find Jan.

# Chapter 15

I found her without any trouble, but she was busy. You could hear Whispering Sands slamming herself against the wings of the loading ramp from a long way away, though I didn't know which pony it was until I got to the van. There was an admiring crowd gathered at a respectful distance, lots of advice from everyone there, and Jan was looking slightly annoyed. Most of the ponies loaded easily, but every once in a while Whispering Sands gave us a hard time.

"Lend me your coat a minute, Cindy," Jan said. I took it off, gave it to her, and she wrapped it around the pony's head. Whispering Sands gave a bored sigh, tapped the ramp with one hoof uncertainly as Jan led her forward, and then walked meekly into the van.

"It's all over, folks," Jan said cheerfully as she came back out of the van. "You can all go home now." She handed me my coat, we waited in silence until the van was ready, and then hurried to the car.

"Crumb was murdered!" I shouted to Jan as we drove out of the show grounds. I had to shout to be heard over the roar of the big van behind us. The road was narrow and hilly. Jan's own van in front of us crept slowly around the sharp bends in the road; the tree branches overhead scraped and banged on its roof and sides. The ponies hated this sound and we followed anxiously, ready to stop and help if one of them got panicky.

"He was murdered." I no longer had to shout. We had turned onto a concrete highway and the vans picked up speed. The engine sounds grew quieter and the huge van behind us passed us with a growl, starting its long journey south.

"It's hard for you," Jan said gently, "but you know it was an accident. No one would want to hurt your pony. It was just sheer chance that moved him into Cat Burglar's stall last night. Alex was lucky, that's all. If Cat had been in that stall when the electric wire came down, he'd have chewed it, just like Crumb, and he'd have been dead instead."

"Exactly." I nodded and watched the van in front of us without seeing it. "I told you Crumb was murdered, only they got the wrong one. It was Cat Burglar who was supposed to be killed." I was astonished at how calm I managed to sound.

"That's nonsense," said Jan. "Why would anyone want to do a thing like that? Surely you don't think a jealous competitor with evil intentions arranged to have that wire slip into the stall?"

"Oh, for gosh sakes, Jan," I said in a strangled voice. "I don't know who actually did it, but I'll bet anything it was Alex's idea."

Jan was silent. I went on stubbornly. "A convenient

accident. Just like the black horse of the Davidsons' that broke his neck last spring. Just like the chestnut that died a couple of months ago. Whatshisname, the jumper with the funny white blaze."

"He died of colic," Jan said.

"Oh, sure," I said. "Colic. Brought on by a pitchfork in the stomach."

Jan's face went white. "That can't be true," she said.

"That's what I said when I heard about it. Angie and Gregory came to tell me about it. They were just wandering around, like little kids do. Like I used to do at these big shows until I learned better. 'They're jumping a horse over hay bales in the aisle of the back tent,' they told me. 'And they're poking him with a pitchfork to make him jump higher.' They even told me which horse it was when we watched the class together a little later that day. They recognized him when he came into the ring."

I glanced at Jan to see if she was listening. "You know something funny? I didn't pay much attention to them because they're just little kids, just as I don't think for one minute that anybody's going to pay any attention to me now. The chestnut horse jumped slowly and carefully, he even won a ribbon. And he was dead the next day. Ruptured stomach, they said. Accidental death. Some colic."

We drove on for a while in silence. "I don't suppose you can prove any of this," Jan said at last.

"Of course not," I said bitterly. "It was weeks before I heard the chestnut horse had died and what he was supposed to have died from. What was I supposed to do, run around waving a little flag, yelling that some insurance company had been cheated again? But I'm not a complete baby. Not after some of the stuff I've seen this summer. I don't care whether you believe me or not. There's something funny the matter with Cat Burglar, he can't feel anything in his left front leg, and maybe *he* was supposed to have the accident last night."

Jan slowed down. She signaled to the van with her lights that everything was all right. The van flashed its lights in answer and Jan swung the station wagon into the parking lot of a Howard Johnson's.

"Come on," she said. "Let's hear the rest of this. You don't talk very often, Cindy, but now you've gotten started, I have the feeling I'd better listen."

We were shown to a booth. Jan leaned forward. "Go on," she said.

I suddenly felt very tired. "I don't really know very much," I said, "and most of this is putting little bits and pieces together. I've seen some pretty peculiar things at some of these big shows. Not just convenient accidents, either. Like the groom I saw giving a horse a shot with a needle one morning. I asked him what he was doing and he nearly had a coronary; he hadn't seen me going by. He told me it was a shot of vitamins and I was dumb enough to think it was wonderful. Vitamins." I nearly choked on a sip of water. "You know what horse it was? The colt of Bold Ruler, fresh off the race track. Everybody had been talking about what lovely manners he had and how quietly he behaved. He won three classes that weekend and he went like a mouse. What kind of stuff do they use on these horses to quiet them down, anyway? You said show horses were tested for drugs."

"They are," said Jan. "A lot of them. But the trouble is that every time the vets find a test for one particular drug, somebody comes up with a new one that's not as easy to trace."

Jan had ordered a cup of tea for me and I stared at the tea bag oozing brown fluid like a bloody wound. At least, that's what it looked like to me, the way I was thinking at the moment. I shuddered and pushed the cup away.

Jan stirred her coffee slowly. "I've told you I used to show my father's horses a few years ago, and I expected things to be pretty much the same when I started showing again last summer. But there've been a lot of changes. Some of them good ones—better quality horses, especially the jumpers, better jumper courses, and an awful lot more prize money—"

"Big money, big trouble," I said, quoting Tim.

"I'm afraid that's right," said Jan. "But it's not just the prize money. It's glory and publicity, too, so some people pay fortunes for horses and demand instant success. Never mind what has to be done to the horses to get it. They don't know, and they don't care, how hard it is to find a good horse, or how long it takes to train and school one so it can go on and get better as the years go by.

"Even in the pony and junior classes, some of the parents today pay the most incredible amounts for show ponies for their kids and they expect to win. Right away. And somehow there always seems to be a trainer or teacher somewhere to tie the new pony's head down with a short martingale, or stick him with a needle full of something to make him quiet, or jazz him up, or make a lame pony look sound—"

She looked into her coffee cup as though she'd never seen it before. "It's a miserable situation. This kind of thing is always hard to stop, in any sport, when people get greedy. The vets are going crazy trying to stop it, and most of the owners and riders and trainers are doing everything they can. But it's all so hard to prove, most of the time—"

Her voice trailed off. "Drugging—funny accidents— if your pony was caught in the middle of something like this, I'll never forgive myself."

"It wasn't your fault!" I stared at her in horror.

"How could you have known? If anybody should have been suspicious, it was me."

It was Jan's turn to look startled. So I told her about seeing her van in Mr. Martin's field and how Crumb and I had been there when Alex had hidden a horse in the old hay barn.

"Could the horse have been Cat Burglar?" I said. "Could Alex have had something done to him there he didn't want anybody to know about, so he could go on jumping and winning a while longer? And then arranged a so-called accident to hide what he had done?"

Jan nodded. "No problem. It wouldn't be the first time something like that's been managed. But it's like the drugging, it's usually hard to prove."

She didn't say anything for a few minutes and then she almost smiled. "You kids sure turn up at the darndest times, don't you? Did Alex know you were there?"

"Gosh, no," I said.

Jan stood up, looking grim again. "Cat Burglar's miracle cure last spring. It would explain a lot of things. Come on, let's go home. I'm going to get in touch with a few people. Maybe we can do something, this time, if we move fast enough."

We got into the car and drove the rest of the way home in silence.

Jan came in to talk to my mother and father. Tim sat quietly and listened with a grim look on his face. I tried to avoid him after Jan had gone. I was afraid he'd say "I told you so," but he didn't. For once in his life he was tactful and kind, and all he said was "I'm sorry," as though he really meant it.

I never found out who Jan called that night, but early the next morning there were two men in dark suits in our living room—one of the men had a badge. They asked me some questions, refused an offer of coffee politely, shook hands with everybody, and drove off as quietly as they had come.

I still couldn't eat. I tried an English muffin, but it stuck horribly in my throat. Crumb's beautiful trophy and Championship ribbon were on the mantelpiece in the living room. I tried putting them away in a drawer, but that only seemed to make things worse, so I brought them out again.

"I want to go to Jan's," I said finally, and Tim was so glad I'd found something to do that he took me over himself on the back of his motorcycle.

There wasn't a sign of Alex or Dan, or any of their stable help. Jan was flying in all different directions trying to get everything done at once. The telephone in the office kept ringing and Alex's horses were banging on their stall doors and kicking the partitions, demanding to be fed.

It was wonderful to be busy. Tim stayed to help. We had no idea how much to feed Alex's horses, so we grained them lightly and gave them a lot of hay, which wouldn't hurt them and would keep them happy until we got things sorted out.

Just as I finished filling the last water bucket, a van rolled into the stable yard. "Hey, Jan!" the driver shouted. "What's all this about Alex trying to zap his own horse at the show?"

"Nobody knows that for sure," said Jan. "It's good to see you, Larry."

"I've come to get Bright Interval back!" Larry swung out of the cab and went to tug at the van doors. "Where's Alex? I've got a message for him from the McKays. All things considered, they said, they'd like their mare to come back to me."

"Have you got that in writing?" Jan looked nervous. "I can't let you take the horse off the place, Larry, and Alex isn't here. I don't know where he is."

"I've got a note from the McKays right in my pocket." Larry handed the envelope to Jan, grinned, and went off, whistling, to get his horse.

Jan read the note and smiled. "Third stall on the left!" she said.

Larry came back a few minutes later leading Bright Interval. He stopped her in the stable yard and went over her legs with anxious care. "Guess she's okay," he said, "but I'll sure be glad to get her away from Alex. I've known him a long time, and even the good horses don't last long with him. What was he up to with Cat Burglar? What was he trying to hide this time?"

"Nobody knows that for sure," Jan repeated firmly. "It's just there was an accident, and there's an investigation . . ."

"Yeah. I heard." Larry shook his head. "Heard some nice kid's pony got it instead. If it wasn't an accident, I hope they run that guy out of the country with a pitchfork—" he glanced at me, patted Bright Interval, and led her tenderly into the van.

Jan helped him with the ramp and waved as he drove off, and then laughed as she saw another van waiting on the road. "I wonder what Alex would say if he came in right now?" she said. "I wonder if anyone's found him yet? There seem to be a lot of people wanting to ask him questions."

The telephone was ringing. Tim ran to answer it and came back to the stable door. "Hey, Jan!" he shouted. "It's the police. They want to know if you've heard anything from Alex!"

Jan threw her hands in the air and went to the phone.

Tim and I cleaned stalls and turned some of the ponies out. Vans and trailers came and went as the word spread and Alex's clients sent for their horses.

Two vets came to see Cat Burglar. I had fed him and groomed him myself. He was a quiet, gentle horse and I was perfectly able to bring him out when the vets came. One doctor had been sent by an insurance company and one by the hunt club where Crumb had died. Jan and I watched. They examined him carefully, but it took them less than a minute to find two small scars on Cat's left front leg.

"No question about it," said one vet crisply. "This horse has been high-nerved." The other doctor nodded sadly. "What a shame," he said. He stroked Cat's shining shoulder and the horse turned his head and nudged the vet's arm gently.

The two doctors took X-rays with a portable machine and went off to make their reports.

I knelt and felt the two tiny, almost invisible scars on Cat's leg. "But Alex turned down half a million dollars for this horse!" I said. "I don't understand."

"He turned it down, didn't he?" said Tim. "More than once, from what you told me. I guess this explains a lot."

"It certainly does," said Jan. "Cat's not worth a penny now. Hardly any insurance company will touch a horse that has been nerved like this, and no vet in the world would pass him as sound. And nobody in the world in their right mind would pay that much money for a horse they couldn't insure. A horse that has been nerved like this can't feel anything at all in his lower leg or hoof. It's an instant cure for lameness, of course, and it's often done to horses to make them comfortable if they're going to be retired and spend the rest of their lives out at pasture.

"But racing or jumping a horse that has been high-nerved is a very cruel and dangerous thing to do. The unsound leg eventually breaks down badly under stress—sooner or later, something terrible will happen and the horse will have to be destroyed."

Jan shook her head sadly. "I guess Alex felt that Cat Burglar's time was running out. Maybe he got nervous. Too much attention was being paid to his horse, too much talk about big money, too much publicity. I wonder if he had this done before he realized how good a horse Cat was, or whether he already knew, and did it anyway, and hoped to cover it up. We'll probably never know. But if Cat had died at the show by chewing through the electric wire, it would have been a very convenient accident, as far as Alex was concerned. No one would have dreamed of looking for the scars on Cat's leg in all the confusion and excitement over the death of such a famous horse.

"A lot of people think that Alex planned the so-called accident, and gambled on the managers of the show repaying him for Cat's death. There'd been so much talk about how much the horse was worth that Alex may well have hoped the show would pay handsomely, without lawsuits and such, just to avoid a lot of bad publicity."

She shrugged her shoulders tiredly. "Poor Cat. Poor Crumb."

Everything stayed in an uproar for days. There were new legal problems and new horse problems every time we turned around. Alex hadn't been found. There was no word from him or from Dan. In the middle of all of this, one of Jan's ponies got a bad case of colic that kept Jan up all night, two nights in a row. The pony survived, but I didn't think Jan was going to; she looked awful.

Two of Alex's horses were left in the stable, other than Cat. One was the hysterical black mare, Cantata, which Alex had shown under a corporation name, and no one seemed to know who she really belonged to. The other was a magnificent bay Trakehner-Thoroughbred cross that had been sent over from Germany and belonged, as Jan discovered after hours of telephoning, to eight different people.

"A kind of syndicate, like a race horse," Jan explained as we looked at the beautiful horse in his stall. "I hate to think what this one's worth. He's done all kinds of winning in Europe. I wish I could track down Alex, just for a minute, to ask him about this horse. From everything I've heard, I don't dare turn him out. He'd probably jump every paddock fence between here and the highway." She sighed wearily. "I'll keep hand-walking him for an hour every day until I get word from his owners. I wouldn't ride him without their permission, but he's got to be exercised."

One of the owners appeared at eleven o'clock that night. Jan was in the stable, checking the sick pony, when the car came racing up the drive. She thought it might be another investigator, or someone again from the police, but it was Colonel Rylander, who owned a part of the big bay horse and was half out of his mind with worry.

Jan made him coffee in the tack room and explained what little she knew about Alex. Colonel Rylander had heard about the fuss all the way in Switzerland, at a horse show there, and had caught the first plane home.

"This horse means more to me than anything else in the world I own," he told Jan. He insisted on getting the horse out of the stall and going over every inch of him in the dim light of the stable aisle. He meant to own all of the horse before the week was out, and before he'd left he'd asked Jan if she'd keep the horse on in her care.

"He said he wants the horse to be shown at Harrisburg, and maybe at the Garden, and definitely at Toronto," she said happily the next day. "It wasn't his idea to send the horse to Alex. He said he would have known better. He'd been an old friend of my father's, as a matter of fact, and was going to look me up when he got back to New York next week. I don't know if that's true or not, but this is one time I'm not going to look a gift horse in the mouth. What an incredible opportunity. Alex may have done me a big favor, after all!"

Cantata, who was always just half a jump ahead of a fit, got to be more and more difficult to handle until it wasn't safe to go near her, even in the stall. Jan worried and fussed over her and finally called Dr. Maxwell, her own vet, who came to look at the wild-eyed mare and shook his head.

"I know this one, all right," he said. "She's been around for years. She's had more different names than the telephone book, but the only one that fits her is trouble. She killed a groom in Chicago a few years back. Alex must have been giving her something in her feed to quiet her down or he'd never have been able to manage her at all. Whatever it was, it's worn off. You'd better stay away from her as much as you can. I hope we hear something from Alex soon. Be careful."

I took care of Cat Burglar myself. A lot of people came to see him. Two members of the Equestrian Team came to talk to Jan and one of them left a check for her to help with her added expenses. Jan protested, but the team member wouldn't listen. "It costs a lot to feed a horse today, and you've got two of them on your hands that don't even belong to you. I don't see anyone rushing over to pick up that crazy Cantata mare. I wonder how Alex ever got stuck with her? And then there's Cat."

He stopped by Cat's stall. "There are so few good ones," he said sadly, "and not nearly enough like this one. With the right kind of care, he might have gone on for years. It's a crime what Alex did to this horse. Have they found him yet?"

Jan shook her head. Rumors, as always, were flying. Someone had seen him at a racetrack in Mexico—someone else was sure they'd seen him with the racing harness horses on Long Island. There'd been nothing illegal about his nerving his own horse, unless he'd had it done to cheat an insurance company, and nobody seemed really to know. There still was no proof that Crumb had not died by accident. All the investigators wanted to do was ask Alex some questions, but it wasn't hard to guess that Alex wasn't anxious to answer them.

We never saw Alex again. Somebody eventually was found who could sign the necessary permission papers, and the vet came and Cantata was put down; the poor angry mare was at last at peace. And a group of professional horsemen and amateur riders arranged a formal retirement ceremony for Cat.

Jan and I spent hours grooming and trimming the big horse until we had him gleaming like patent leather. We braided his mane and tail for the last time and took him over to the show grounds one bright and glorious afternoon. Just before the start of the big jumping class, the ringmaster blew a call on his horn. The wide white gate swung open and Jan rode Cat into the ring, and I walked in beside them.

The announcer read the list of classes and championships the horse had won. Cat Burglar stood quietly on the short grass in the center of the ring and looked at the banks of flowers and gaily painted fences of the course around him—fences he would never jump again, though he couldn't have known that.

Jan dismounted. We took off Cat's saddle and

bridle and I buckled his dark leather halter in place. The ringmaster slipped a soft blue cooler over Cat's back—it had the horse's name on it, and the name and date of the show, in white block letters on one side.

The president of the horse show and his wife placed a banner of red and white roses across Cat's shoulders —it reached below his knees—and as they stepped back away from the horse, the silent crowd of spectators rose and gradually started applause that grew to a roar as the band broke into the triumphant strains of "Bonnie Dundee."

Cat arched his gleaming neck and pranced at the end of the lead shank. I offered Jan the lead shank with a smile, but with an answering smile she moved back a step and it was I who led Cat around the ring and through the white gates for his very last time.

I'm afraid I wept a little. A lot of people did. People crowded around the big horse offering him sugar and carrots, patting him shyly on his neck as he accepted the gifts gracefully. Jan answered what questions she could about Cat and his history. The gleaming brass chain on the end of the lead shank twinkled and chinked softly as the horse moved his head.

Out on the field the show jumpers were warming up for their class. The gray stallion that had been

second to Cat in the Gold Cup was there and his
scarlet-coated rider raised his hand in salute as we
led Cat away from the ring.

The band stopped playing. There was a pause, and
the ringmaster lifted his gleaming coaching horn and
blew the call for the jumping class. Spectators settled
back in their seats and the first horse jogged into the
ring. Cat stopped, flung his head high, and turned to
look back. I couldn't help wondering if he wanted
to be with the others, waiting for his class. Jan took
the lead shank from my hand, clucked softly to the
horse, and led him to the van.

In silence we took off his ribbon of roses, folded
his new cooler, and buckled his plaid stable sheet
into place. Jan put on his shipping bandages and
loaded him into the van to go home.

Cat came home to me. It is lovely to have his lean,
wise head looking over the door of Crumb's stall
and he goes out with Mr. Martin's cows in nice
weather, just as Crumb used to do. The vet and the
blacksmith come often to keep an eye on him and
they both say he's doing nicely.

I ride Cat bareback now and then, just with a
halter and rope and we wander slowly around the
fields and through the woods where I had such a
wonderful time with Crumb. Of course Cat doesn't

jump any more, but as I ride by, the walls don't look as big to me as they did, which is not Mr. Martin's fault, but my own—Jan has opened up Alex's wing of her stable and she is teaching me to help school her growing number of hunters and jumpers and, as I'm slowly getting to be a better rider, the walls don't look as high.

School started a few weeks ago. The summer shows are over. Sam, the Welsh pony, along with Whispering Sands and many of the other show ponies, has been turned out to rest and play in the pastures for the next few months. Jan is causing quite a stir winning with the gigantic bay German horse, much to Colonel Rylander's delight.

He comes to the stables as often as he can and we stand in the wide white ring as Jan works with his magnificent horse and he tells me of the great jumpers he's known in the past—horses in countries all over the world. Horses I've read about and dreamed about ever since I can remember.

Democrat. Tosca. Foxhunter. Halla, Circus Rose, and the little bay Mexican horse, Arete. Idle Dice and Good Twist. "These have been some of my favorites," said the Colonel with respect and admiration, in the same kind of voice I've heard people use when they talk about Cat. "They make fools of the petty and bring glory to the sport."

I wonder if Alex saw the picture of Jan, riding the German horse, on the cover of *Sports Illustrated* last week. They won the Puissance class at Harrisburg and the stone wall was almost eight feet high. They were tying the world's record for height when the picture was taken.

I taped the picture on the wall in my room with the rest of the fantastic collection of photographs it's taken me years to scrounge from various places—I have one of Democrat, and a spectacular one of Pat Smythe on her Tosca, and the little gray mare's knees are tucked right up under her chin in mid-air over a triple bar. I have one of Sloopy over the water jump at the Olympics and one of Good Twist at Aachen and I have two each of Nautical and Snowman, who were so famous they even had movies made about them.

And underneath, in a row by themselves, there's Jan winning on the big bay horse at Harrisburg. There's a color portrait of Cat at his retirement ceremony, wearing his banner of red and white roses, and the picture the newspaper photographer took of Crumb.

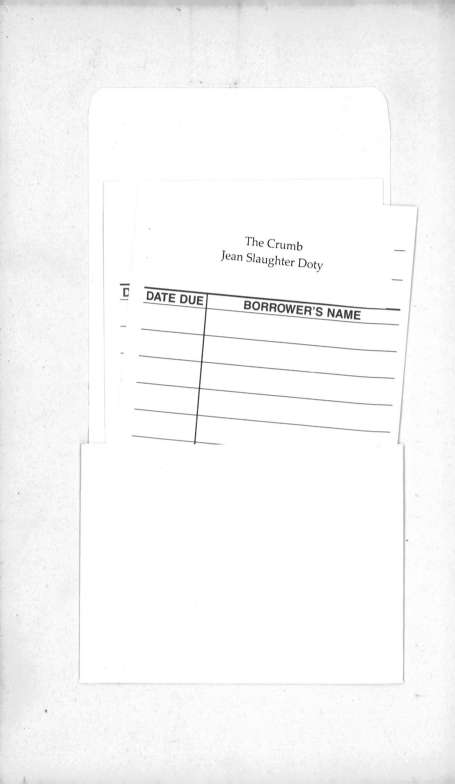

The Crumb
Jean Slaughter Doty

| DATE DUE | BORROWER'S NAME |
|----------|-----------------|
|          |                 |
|          |                 |
|          |                 |
|          |                 |